Mischief
and
Malice

Mischief
and
Malice

Berthe Amoss

LIZZIE
SKURNICK
BOOKS

Brooklyn, New York

Printed in the United States
Reissue Edition
10 9 8 7 6 5 4 3 2 1

Please direct inquiries to:
Lizzie Skurnick Books
an imprint of Ig Publishing
392 Clinton Avenue #1S
Brooklyn, NY 11238
www.igpub.com

ISBN: 978-1-939601-44-5 (hardcover)
ISBN: 978-1-939601-45-2

Mischief
and
Malice

One

The thing you have to understand is that besides memorizing your catechism it really works if you believe it. Like the Communion of Saints part. "I believe in the Communion of Saints," the Catechism says, and we're all suppose to be saints, not just those they've got statues of in the Church, but you, me, and all the dead people who have gone before, excluding, of course, those who've descended into hell.

The communion part means communication—so you've got this kind of giant telephone system where you can call up from New Orleans all the way to one of the saints in heaven and say, "Please, Aunt Eveline, you remember how I prayed for the repose of your soul at mass on Sunday? Well, now I need some help from you. There's this boy, called Leonard McCloskey, who is captain of the Jesuit football team and a very good Catholic, Aunt Eveline! He kneels and crosses himself before every game and his team almost always wins unless it's playing another Catholic team who've also knelt and crossed themselves, which I'm sure presents God with a problem. But the point is it's perfectly all right for me to like Leonard McCloskey. The only thing is I don't know if he likes me. In fact, I'm not sure he knows who I am, Aunt Eveline, so if you could just ask God to let Leonard notice me, I'll take care of the rest."

I said this prayer on Monday last week just before Saturday's Jesuit game and the answer came back with telegraphic speed. First, Tom, who was away at school, wrote in his letter, "I sure hope Jesuit wins. Tell Leonard good luck for me." Now that might not seem on the surface to be the answer to a prayer but since Tom usually doesn't write about anything except his dog and how he wishes the United States would declare war on Hitler, I could tell it was divine intervention. So just before the game, I stood at the entrance to the locker room in the stadium, and when the team came out, I pushed forward as Leonard passed by and called, "Tom says 'good luck!'" and Leonard looked me and said, "Thanks, Addie!"

Addie! He called me by my name! I love the way he says my name, with a sort of lilt: 'Ad-dee,' and a very small smile playing at the edge of his mouth. I can't wait for him to say 'Ad-dee' again, and I take this to be a direct, affirmative response and encouragement from God and you, Aunt Eveline, that you both approve of Leonard. Thanks, Aunt Eveline! Keep up the good work; I'm counting on you!

I miss Aunt Eveline because she raised me and I am pleased to have this direct means of communication of saints so that we can stay in touch. I am very sorry not to still be living at Three Twenty Audubon Street with her, especially since now I have to live next door at my Aunt Toosie and

Uncle Henry's house with my hateful cousin, Sandra Lee. I can't wait to go away to college and become a famous artist. Aunt Toosie said, "Addie, dear, Eveline wanted you to go to the very best art school. How do you feel about going to Newcomb with Sandra Lee?"

"I'm not sure about Newcomb, Aunt Toosie," I answered. I've got to make sure wherever I go is a million miles from wherever Sandra Lee goes. Actually, I've been considering Smith, which I think, is near West Point with good-looking cadets, but I don't know if Smith has an art school and I'm not sure we have the money for me to go that far away. Thank goodness I don't have to solve the college problem this year. The Leonard problem needs all of my attention before I can concentrate on art.

Maybe I should make up something else Tom said to tell him like "Tom said for me to tell you 'Congratulations!'" if the team wins, of course, or if they lose, "Tom said for me to tell you 'Tough Luck!'" Then Leonard would have to say "Thanks, Ad-dee!"

No, he wouldn't. He could say, "Tom didn't say that; you just made it up because you're boy crazy. I wish your pretty cousin, Sandra Lee, would talk to me instead of you." He could say that to me and not even say my name once and I'd deserve it for lying, so I'll just turn the whole thing back to you, Aunt Eveline. I need a little more help and I'll be praying for the repose of your soul again on Sunday, so do you think you could arrange a situation where Leonard would have to speak to me first? Thanks in advance, Aunt Eveline!

I had just made that fervent prayer, and I happened to be standing in the pantry next to the kitchen with my hand on an unopened jar of blackberry jam, when I heard the screen door slam, and then sobs.

"Mabel! What's wrong?" Aunt Toosie cried as Tom's mother sobbed louder. "What's the matter, dear?!" I froze and listened.

"Louis is the matter!" cried Aunt Mabel. "Toosie, Louis is coming home! He'll be here any minute! He phoned from Mobile!"

"My God, Mabel! I can't believe it!" Aunt Toosie yelled. "How does he have the nerve?!"

It was too late to make my presence known. It was also too interesting. Louis is Tom's father who left when Tom was an infant, and no one had seen or heard from him since then.

"Disappeared into the blue," Tom's Uncle Malvern said, and moved in with Tom and Aunt Mabel to take care of them. But Uncle Malvern has turned out to be more like another child than the man of the house. It is Aunt Mabel and Tom who take care of Uncle Malvern while he works on his invention, the Perpetual Motion Machine.

In between sobs Aunt Mabel was saying, "What shall I do? What does he expect of me? Where has he been? I've wired Tom. I don't want to see that man again! Oh, Toosie, yes, I do! In all these years, I've never really stopped loving Louis!"

"Now, now, then, Mabel darling, of course, you still love him. You are such a loving person and, of course, you want to see him, but Mabel, listen to me, don't give an inch! No matter what he says! You know he has a silver tongue and only cares for himself and money. Don't give him an inch, Mabel!"

Aunt Toosie went on and on with useless advice about inches. I thought how much better it would be for Aunt Mabel to read that book that Sandra Lee has, *Dearest*, which tells you everything and I mean everything about what to do and say in any situation you can imagine.

Aunt Toosie was still chattering away about inches and Aunt Mabel about bygones as they left the kitchen for Aunt Mabel's to fix up the guest room for Louis.

That's another thing about getting old: most people lose sight of the important things and get bogged down in stuff that really doesn't matter. Why don't they fix up Aunt Mabel instead of a room? She needs a new hair-do desperately. Even I could have told her that without reading *Dearest*. And she needs to change the expression on her face, which looks like the illustration of St. Agatha in *Early Christian Martyrs*.

I wandered into the kitchen to get bread and peanut butter for my jam. Tom's father. Louis. What did he look like now? I remembered a snapshot of him with my mother.

He was certainly handsome then: tall, with wavy blond hair and a kind of devil-may-care smile. Something like Tom but much, much more sophisticated and interesting-looking. I didn't blame Aunt Mabel for still caring about Louis. If I were in her place, I wouldn't worry about giving inches.

I decided to consult *Dearest*. I ran upstairs to Sandra Lee's room where she keeps it sandwiched between her collection of Nancy Drew mysteries. Sandra Lee has made a brown paper cover exactly like the ones we made for our school books, and she's written "Little Lives of Saints for Little People" on the outside so that Aunt Toosie won't open it. *Dearest* has sample letters and conversations for every stage of a love affair that would be pretty embarrassing if your mother caught you reading it. But it is so clear that you never have to be at a loss for something to write or tongue-tied if you can remember the right page. For instance, on page 76 in the chapter called "Going Steady but not Ready," it tells how you can encourage a boy without "letting him go too far." I turned to page 96 in the chapter called "Getting Heady and Ready" where it tells "how to encourage a reluctant suitor and bring him to the brink of matrimony." Unfortunately, page 96 had taken a lot of wear and literal tear before Sandra Lee got it and a large corner with crucial facts was missing. What was left read: "At this point, one must be careful not to ___for instead of encouraging a proposal, ___might lead a potential fiancé to

thereby placing the potential fiancé into the position of___.
On the other hand, by___the fiancé may___and this cannot
fail to bring the suitor to his knees."

Important words like "kissing" and "petting" were
bound to be in there, plus the ominous phrase "going all
the way." It was just a matter of fitting the missing phrases
into the right blanks. We did it all the time in school, things
like, God is___. Choose one of the following:

    a) three Gods in one person

    b) one God in three persons

    c) invisible, etc.

I was trying to fill in the blanks for page 96 and
wondering if Aunt Mabel was too old for this kind of
advice when Sandra Lee burst yelling, "Uncle Malvern's
tried to hang himself on his Perpetual Motion Machine!
And Tom's father has come home! He's here! *In a uniform*!"

I could see Sandra Lee was pleased to be the one with
dramatic information about Tom's family.

Sandra Lee looks her best when she's excited. Her
eyes, already big and round, get rounder and her perfectly
shaped, little mouth is parted slightly. She was waiting for
me to say something like "Good Heavens!", so I lowered
my eyelids and raised my eyebrows which makes me look
slightly bored and said, "I knew Tom's father was arriving. I
sincerely hope Uncle Malvern's effort was in vain."

"And Tom's on his way home too! Now!"

"He is?! My God!" I cried.

"Don't take the name of the Lord in vain," she said. "Mother's already helping Aunt Mabel cook a big pot of gumbo. We could bring over something."

"We can bring the leftover cookies I made yesterday," I said.

"You forgot the sugar."

"I'll dust them with confectioner's," I said. "Hurry up!"

A million things criss-crossed my mind. First, I was dying to see what Tom's father looked like. Second, Tom would deliver his own messages now, and I wouldn't even have an excuse to talk to Leonard any more. Third and worst of all, everybody considered me Tom's girl, but it was really a process of elimination instead of a romance; Tom had never had a girlfriend and I'd never had a boyfriend, and we'd grown up next door to each other and raised the same dog. It was positively infuriating to be linked romantically with a tall skinny boy whose main interests were football, a mangy dog, and a war on the other side of the world. I'd never get anywhere with Leonard McClosky now.

Sandra Lee reached in the cookie tin and pulled out what was left of the cookies I'd made. Spread out and sprinkled with powdery sugar, they filled the plate and looked nice.

"Sandra Lee, did they say how Uncle Malvern tried to hang himself?"

"He didn't exactly try. He was sitting on top of the Perpetual Motion Machine and fell, and on the way down he got caught in the old shower curtain he'd rigged up to keep water from splashing on the floor. He's okay now."

You might know the news wasn't as dramatic as Sandra Lee wanted me to think.

We hurried over to Tom's house, two doors away. Aunt Eveline's sweet olive tree was in bloom and the tiny white flowers sent their heavy, sweet smell down the whole block. I tried to see into the living room window of my old house as we went by, but the curtains were drawn. I noticed the Communion of Saints telephone was ringing and thought I heard Aunt Eveline saying "Addie, what goes on at Three Twenty Audubon Street is no longer any of your business, and if you're going over to Tom's house out of vulgar, common curiosity and not Christian Charity for Tom's mother you'd best turn around and get on with your own affairs such as your artistic career."

"Sandra Lee," I said, "do you think Aunt Mabel really wants us to come over?"

"Of course," said Sandra Lee primly. Besides *Dearest*, she has a book of etiquette by Emily Post, which she has memorized better than her catechism. "You always go to a friend's house in times of crisis," Sandra Lee said. "To help. You can be helpful talking to Uncle Malvern about his invention and taking him off Aunt Mabel's hands."

That was the last thing I wanted to do and Sandra Lee knew it.

"Why don't *you* talk to Uncle Malvern?" I said as we

came around the side of Tom's house. It was too late: there sat Uncle Malvern on the back porch, his grey head in his hands. He looked up, sighed, and smiled when he saw Sandra Lee's golden curls bouncing in the sunlight. He didn't even notice me.

"You look just like Pasie, Sandra Lee!" he said.

The old feeling of helpless envy washed over me. Sandra Lee looked like my beautiful mother and I didn't.

Worse yet, Sandra Lee could pass for eighteen. I, on the other hand, was still Sister Maurice's first choice for the role of Joseph in the Christmas play.

"Oh, thank you so much, Uncle Malvern!" said Sandra Lee sweetly. "Addie here has come over to talk to you and I'll just run in and give Aunt Mabel these cookies we made for her."

Sandra Lee maneuvers like a tank and there I was, stuck with Uncle Malvern. He finally tore his eyes away from her and said, "Oh, hello there, Addie. Nice of you to come. Have a seat."

He patted the step next to him. Uncle Malvern had once been very handsome but the only way you could tell that was from my mother's old snapshots marked "Mal." Now his face was puffy and red, and his body pudgy. He loved my mother all of his life and that was why he'd stayed a bachelor and drank all the time. At least, that was what Aunt Toosie thought.

"Well!" said Uncle Malvern in that jolly way grownups use with children. "I know you'll be pleased to know Tom's coming home tonight!"

I don't know what made me react, whether it was Sandra Lee's maneuver or knowing that I'd already committed at least one venial sin coming over here and I might as well go for broke.

"No," I blurted out. "I'm not glad Tom's coming home!"

The minute I said it, I was sorry.

I was about to apologize to Uncle Malvern who was staring at me in a stunned way when he said, "You know, you look like your mother too! When she got mad! Or do you think I've gotten so old and stupid that every young girl looks like my poor lost love?"

"Oh, Uncle Malvern, you're not old and stupid!" I couldn't help feeling sorry for him. "Look at your invention. No one stupid could invent a Perpetual Motion Machine."

"It doesn't work," he said sadly.

"Tom says it has the potential to work."

"Does he?" said Uncle Malvern hopefully.

"Oh, yes," I said. "Tom says that in theory you are perfectly correct."

This cheered Uncle Malvern so much that he talked on and on about his machine that had grown bigger every time I'd seen it until it took up almost his whole room, reaching to the ceiling and crowding his bed into a corner.

I had stopped listening and was wondering how I could tactfully get up and go home when a tall man dressed in uniform walked out of the kitchen. Even if I hadn't known it was Tom's father, I'd have recognized Louis from the man in the snapshot with my mother. He didn't look any different or old at all. He was still very handsome and had the bluest eyes I have ever seen. I went all embarrassed and stupid, the way I always do, and, having no poise whatsoever, jumped up, which a lady is not supposed to do for any man according to Sandra Lee's etiquette book, and said, of course, the wrong thing:

"Hello, Colonel," is what I said.

He smiled and held out his hand.

"You look too much like your beautiful mother not to be Addie," he answered. "I'm not a Colonel; I'm a Sergeant in the Salvation Army and I'm home at last." He smiled again. "I hope I'm not too late to miss completely being Tom's father, and a friend of Pasie's lovely daughter."

I had never heard a more beautiful speech. I understood what Aunt Mabel meant when she said that Louis had "a silver tongue." I knew that Louis was not supposed to be completely sincere, and I knew too that Tom hated him, but I was bowled over just the same. I tried to remember what *Dearest* says you should say on meeting a potential boyfriend but my mind went blank.

"Excuse me," I said. "I don't know the difference between uniforms but yours is very becoming."

This time I got a big smile, which had to be sincere because his eyes smiled too. "Thank you, Addie. That's very kind of you. Say! I know Tom would like it if you were at the train when he gets in tomorrow night. Would you like to meet him with me? He gets in at nine."

"Oh, yes!" I said. "I'd love to go with you. To meet Tom!"

I concentrated on my facial expression which I hoped would show how sincerely interested I was in seeing my old friend, Tom, and not reveal how anxious I was to be with Louis.

It wasn't until later at home I wondered if Louis was afraid to meet Tom alone.

"Of course he is," said Aunt Eveline clear as a bell. "Stay home and mind your business."

"It is my business," I answered under my breath. "Tom is my friend. And—and Louis is interested in me. I can tell."

"Interested in you? A child?!"

"I'm fourteen!"

"And he's well over forty!"

"So what?" I had never dared to use that expression to Aunt Eveline.

"You are playing with fire, Adelaide! It's time you tamed that overactive imagination of yours and faced reality!" she said. "You have the potential of being a fine artist someday, but it requires dedication, hard work, and training."

"I know." I said under my breath. Aunt Eveline's angry words stayed in my mind as she swept out of it.

Two

"Where are you going?" Sandra Lee asked suspiciously. She had come down the hall so quietly I hadn't heard her. She was staring at my curly hair.

"Out," I said, putting the final touches on my face.

"It's a school night," said Sandra Lee.

"So what?" I asked.

"And your lipstick is purple."

"My lipstick is Ripe Plum and Louis says I look like my mother too. So there!"

"Louis?! Since when do you call Tom's father by his first name?"

"Since yesterday when he invited me to go out with him."

"Out with him?! He's a married man!"

"He is not! He may not be exactly divorced, but he's been gone too long to be married. I heard Uncle Henry say so."

"Emily Post says…"

"I don't care what Emily Post says! I'm going to meet Tom." I picked up my purse, did the trick with my lids and eyebrows and flounced out. At least, I tried to flounce, but Sandra Lee is an expert on the last word, and just before I slammed the front door, I heard her scream, "If you think you look like your mother, you're wrong! You look like Medusa with those dumb curls snaking around your face!"

That is what I mean about Sandra Lee. She hits the nail right on the head when it comes to what to say for every occasion. I already knew the results of an hour's work with the curling iron were disappointing. In the first place, my hair is almost black instead of pale, pale yellow, and in the second place, no matter how my hair looks, my nose is straight instead of turned up. Still, I hadn't felt so bad about my looks until Sandra Lee compared me to the goddess with snakes for hair.

It was already eight-thirty and I didn't have time to work on myself any more. Besides, I couldn't go back inside and let Sandra Lee know I cared what she said. I went to the water faucet at the side of the house, turned it on full, and stuck my head under. The cool water felt delicious after the tortures of the curling iron. I let it run and rubbed my head hard. I suppose I got carried away by the sound of the running water; anyway, I was singing "Roll, Jordan" when I heard a man laughing.

I gasped, choked, and banged my head on the faucet straightening up. There was Louis.

"Oh, Addie," he said between fits of laughter, "you're marvelous! I haven't enjoyed anyone so much in a long time. I …" more laughter. His laugh was contagious and I forgot to be embarrassed and laughed with him.

"I was washing out the curls because I look like Medusa," I said.

"You're absolutely right. Curls are wrong for your kind of beauty." He touched my wet head and said, "They should have named you something very Spanish, like Dolores— yes, that's it—you look like Dolores Del Rio."

Right then and there, I fell in love. I'm not talking about puppy love. Nothing like Leonard. And absolutely as far as possible away from my platonic relationship with Tom. I mean really head over heels into real love, for the very first time in my whole life. Standing in the warm, honeysuckle night, a full moon shining down on me, with a mature man, I knew this was different.

How old was he? Could he really be forty already? If he was about twenty-four when Tom was born, he was about forty now. Maybe he was still only thirty-nine and a half. Thirty-nine and a half, and fifteen next year. That wasn't too bad. It must have happened before, and he'd only be forty-four when I was twenty.

"Come on, Addie, don't just stand there dripping. We're late," he said, handing me his handkerchief. "Dry your hair a little." I hadn't even noticed my hair was sopping wet. "Not that it makes any difference how your hair looks, because I'm sure Tom will think you're lovely just as you are now."

I yearned to tell him it didn't matter to me what Tom thought as long as I looked like my favorite movie star to him.

"This car belongs to the Army," said Louis as we walked to a battered old Ford. His hand was on my elbow guiding me. I had never been helped into a car except when Aunt Eveline died and the undertaker shoved me into the long black limousine they made us ride in. "They lent me a car to come home to New Orleans," Louis added, going around to the driver's seat. "The Army is very understanding."

I loved the way Louis talked to me as though I were his age. "Yes, a gentleman needs a car," I replied.

"I'm glad you consider me a gentleman, Addie. That's more than some people do. I meant to say, though, that the Army understands I need to get my house in order, so to speak, before I can do my best work for them."

Louis looked at me as though I should say something else, but I couldn't think of anything. He put his foot on the accelerator, which gave a yelp like Pumpkin barking, and the car lunged forward.

"I'm not much of a driver," said Louis.

"Oh, you're a wonderful driver! It's the car's fault, I'm sure," I answered.

"You're very kind, Addie, and it's a good thing for me that you are. I need your help with Tom." Louis said this in such a sincere way, I was positive he had forgotten to use his silver tongue.

"I'll do anything I can, Louis," I answered.

As we drove past Three Twenty Audubon Street, we both looked at it. In the dark, and behind the sycamore trees that lined the street, it looked like it had before it was modernized; it looked like home to me.

"You miss Three Twenty?" Louis asked.

"Yes," I said.

I could never think of Aunt Toosie's as home. It was newer and much cozier, a grey-blue cottage, trimmed in what we call gingerbread, wood cut out in a lacy pattern and painted snow-white. Aunt Toosie had trained a Confederate Jasmine vine up a trellis and it made the whole front porch smell sweet. Inside, everything was "Early American," Aunt Toosie said, although the furniture was only about ten years old. But it wasn't home to me, even though it looked like something in a book.

Three Twenty Audubon Street had also looked like something in a book—by Edgar Allen Poe. Everything had been old-fashioned, just the way my grandparents had fixed it up. "Victorian", they called it, for the Queen who sat on the English throne in the nineteenth century. The heavy furniture had been covered in dark upholstery. Thick curtains designed to keep out light and hold old musty smells opened up only to reveal more curtains made of lace and forever in need of mending or cleaning. There were little doilies and china figures everywhere. Dust catchers, Aunt Toosie called them. Not that Aunt Eveline and Nini, who worked for us, hadn't kept every bit of the house spic and span.

"It's funny," Louis was saying, "but when I was away I

used to think of Three Twenty more than my own home.
I spent a lot of time there, many happy afternoons and
evenings with your Uncle Ben, who was my friend. Did you
know that?"

"No," I said.

So many people had lived at Three Twenty Audubon
Street besides me and Aunt Eveline. I could hardly
remember her brother, my Uncle Ben. "This place is the
repository of bygone years," Aunt Eveline used to say
happily, groping her way around the living room.

"I can almost see your Papa," Nini would add, pausing
in her dusting to gaze into the darkest corner of the room
where my grandfather's huge mahogany-and-mohair chair
stood like a throne. "I sees him sitting there, reading his
paper, nodding, 'cause he's getting sleepy, jumping awake
when he hears you come in the room. 'Eveline! Fetch my
cane! I'm going for a stroll on the levee!'"

Nini and Aunt Eveline would go on like that all morning
as they traveled with the cleaning equipment through every
room of the house, stirring up dust and calling up ghosts
that had once lived at Three Twenty.

"An old couple moved out last week and a new family
just moved in," I said to Louis. "A man and his wife and a
girl my age."

"Is she a friend of yours?"

"Not really. I don't know her yet. I think she may be
a little older than I am. The postman told me about her."

Norma Jean was the girl's name. I knew that much. "I think she has my old room," I added trying to keep the envy out of my voice.

When Aunt Eveline died and I moved to Aunt Toosie's, Nini had helped Aunt Toosie bring a few of my things to her house, but Aunt Toosie didn't have room or even want the heavy old furniture and dark oil paintings. "Give it all to the Salvation Army," Uncle Henry had said. Four truckloads of stuff, everything I have grown up with, were carted away. I had watched the men stagger down the front steps with the grandfather clock. Its bong had once scared me to death, but that day, it seemed to be calling for help, chiming sadly as it was jogged along. After the clock came my mother's trunk, and even though Aunt Toosie had tenderly unpacked it and brought the contents to her house, it still was unbearable to see the trunk tossed in a truck. The only thing left in the house was the giant-size armoire too big to fit down the narrow attic stairs. Aunt Eveline had used it for storage and Aunt Toosie was supposed to go through it and take what she wanted, but it was full of junk and Aunt Toosie had never gotten around to it. The Three Twenty I knew was gone. Aunt Eveline was dead and Nini was semi-retired and only working now and then when she was needed. She lived in the country, waiting for the day her niece and my friend, Holly, would visit from her unhappy home in Chicago.

"Addie," Louis interrupted my reverie. "I really meant it

when I said I needed your help. Will you help me?"

"Oh, yes, Louis, I'll do anything I can but—"

"But what?"

"But how could I help *you*?"

"Well, for one thing, you could get Tom to—well, I can't expect too much. I mean I can't expect him to love me, but if he could bring himself to forgive me for what I did, leaving him and his mother. Then maybe after a time—well, I guess that would be all I could hope for! Forgiveness."

"Oh, Louis, I'm sure he'll *love* you—after a while—the minute he knows how nice you really are. Anybody would!" I realized that I'd practically told him I loved him, and I could feel myself blushing in the dark. If I couldn't say the right thing, why couldn't I at least learn to keep my mouth shut?

"Tom has every right to refuse to even see me," Louis continued. "I can understand that. That's where you come in, Addie. If you let him know I'm human, not some monster, and that I deeply regret my mistake—if you think I'm all right, then maybe he'll give me a chance. Do you see what I am?"

"Oh yes! Of course!" I said.

But what I saw was Tom thinking I was siding with his father against him and his mother, and suddenly, I was not nearly so sure that meeting Tom with Louis was such a great idea.

I was even less sure when the train pulled into the

station with a lot of clanging and puffing steam. The conductor hanging on the steps signaled the engineer to stop and I panicked. What was I doing standing here with Louis, meeting Tom's train? It wasn't my business. It was all I could do not to run for all I was worth. Oh, Aunt Eveline, how do I get into such scrapes? Aunt Eveline declined to answer.

If I live to be a hundred, I will never forget the expression on Tom's face when he got off the train. In the first place, I'd forgotten how grown up he was, or maybe he'd grown more since I saw him three months before. He looked a lot like Louis. In fact, he looked exactly like Louis, only younger.

"Tom!" I said, surprised by the resemblance.

He saw me and started to smile; he was getting out of the train and had one foot on the step when he saw Louis. He must have felt he was seeing himself as he would look in twenty-five years. Tom's expression froze, and he tripped and fell. Louis rushed forward to help him up, but Tom was on his feet and gave him a shove with his shoulder, a look of pure hate on his face. Louis drew back as though he'd been slapped, and good old Addie, ready with the wrong word, cried, "Oh Tom, he's your father!"

Tom took a deep breath and said quietly, "Hello, Addie." Then he turned to Louis and said, "Hello."

Tom's face was white. He looked like Pumpkin when he's been slapped. He didn't seem able to tear his eyes away from his father, and Louis was staring at him, both waiting

29

to see what the other would do. I couldn't stand it.

"Oh, please don't fight!" I said.

It was stupid because they were both too grown up to solve their problems that way, but it broke the ice. Tom turned to pick up the suitcase he'd dropped when he fell.

"Come on," Louis said without looking at either of us. "I have a car."

We had to walk single file out of the train station because it was so crowded with another train pulling out and people rushing around.

"All aboard!" the conductor shouted, and I wished with all my heart I could jump on that train and go somewhere— anywhere away from Tom and Louis and the awful tension between them.

By the time we reached the car, Louis had turned cheerful again. "Tom," he said, "can you squeeze in front with Addie so you won't be alone in the back?"

"Yes, sir," said Tom coldly.

"Don't call me 'sir,'" Louis said in the same cheerful tone, "I'm your father!"

It was a mistake. Much too soon. I could have told him that. If he wanted Tom to love him, he'd have to *do* something. Nothing he said, no matter how silvery his tongue, would make a bit of difference with Tom. Why didn't I think to tell Louis that when he asked for help? He didn't know Tom the way I did and he kept making the same stupid mistakes, talking as though he were a normal father who came home every night. It didn't work, and one look at the thin line of Tom's mouth told me he was making Tom hate him all the more.

I tried to think of something to say to change the subject. If only I'd had Sandra Lee's etiquette book. *Dearest* was a little too intimate for the occasion but I could have found the right phrase in Emily Post. Better yet, if only I'd had the sense to mind my business and stay home, I wouldn't have a problem. I sat there tongue-tied while poor Louis hung himself.

Finally in desperation I said, "Tom, I read in the newspaper where Roosevelt made a speech and said all that matters is who fires the last shot." I hadn't exactly read it but Uncle Henry had and then announced it to everyone at the breakfast table.

"Yes," said Tom, forgetting he was supposed to be mad, "and Hitler answered him and said 'the last battalion in the field will be German.' If I were the president, I'd send troops over there right now and put an end to that maniac!"

"He can't do that, Tom," said Louis patiently. "The president needs congressional—"

"I know what the president needs," Tom interrupted rudely. "He needs congressional permission to go to war. If I were president, I'd figure a way around that, but since I'm just a kid in school, I don't even have a say in who invades my own house."

I gasped and stole a glance at Louis. He didn't say a

word, but he looked startled, then very angry. No one said another thing until we got home. Then Louis said sternly, "Tom, walk Addie to her door. Then go see your mother. She's waiting for you in her room."

"I know what to do," Tom said rudely. "You park and I'll walk home."

With that he turned his back on his father, and we walked to my door, Tom striding ahead of me. I had never seen him so angry.

"Tom?" I tried.

"Goodnight, Addie," he said.

There went my one and only friend. I slunk into the house. Sandra Lee was listening to the radio in the living room and I got up the stairs without her hearing me. The evening had been a gigantic flop. Some stupid to think I could get anywhere with a forty-five-year-old man when I couldn't even make a dumb football player say more than "Hello" to me! And now, the only friend I had, hated me as much as he hated his father. I was a traitor and he knew it.

I looked in the mirror and saw that half the curls had survived the Jordan. Dolores?! I looked like Albert Einstein. Tears came to my eyes and I thought, oh, Aunt Eveline, why did you have to die before I grew up all the way? Please don't send me any more penance, because I've done enough to cover dozens of sins I haven't even gotten around to committing yet.

I turned off the light and went to the window. I could

see my very own old room at Three Twenty only about fifteen feet away. Oh, how I wished I were there still, snug in my bed, too young to have a love life, with Aunt Eveline about to tuck me in and tell me what a great artist I would be some day. I'd been crying a long time in the dark, staring over at my window, when suddenly I could see in. The door to the lighted hall opened, and there in the window, silhouetted through ruffled organdy curtains, the kind I'd always wanted and never had, I saw a girl. I only saw her for a moment and heard a woman's voice carry across: "Don't forget your medicine, Norma Jean. Goodnight." And the door shut out the light.

Three

The next morning when Uncle Henry knocked on my door to wake me for school, I discovered my head felt like a cannon ball, my nose was stopped up, and my throat was scratchy from gasping air through my mouth.

"I'm sick," I croaked at Uncle Henry. Aunt Toosie came to my room on the double. She felt my head and popped a thermometer in my mouth.

"Close your mouth, dear. Don't bite the thermometer!"

"I can't breathe through my nose!" I cried in a panic.

"Don't talk! You'll bite the thermometer!" She took it out. "It registers one whole degree above normal already! Stay in bed and I'll call the doctor. What in the world could you have?"

I knew what I had. I had a terrible cold from driving around with a wet head. Besides the cold symptoms, I had a miserable all-over feeling of hating myself.

I tried to tune in on Aunt Eveline, but she was out. If only I could go back in time. Instead of wasting my days plotting how to get Leonard to notice me, I would answer Tom's letter. I would tell him all the things he wanted to know, like how his dog was getting along. I would, of course, have been paying more attention to Pumpkin, taking him for a daily walk and giving him bones, and I'd tell Tom how much the football team needed him back, how Harold said he was the best wide receiver they'd ever had, and I'd tell him how happy his mother was that he was doing so well in school up there, and how contented his Uncle Malvern was with the progress he was making on his invention. Naturally, I would be able to say I'd visited Uncle Malvern as often as I could when I wasn't working at my drawing, practicing to be a famous artist.

"Remorse," said Aunt Eveline.

"Remorse?"

"Remorse is closely akin to self-pity." How often Aunt Eveline's words had blown past me unnoticed as a breeze. "If you don't change your ways, what good is remorse?"

"I will change my ways! Aunt Eveline, I'll reform! I'll put on a new spirit just like Sister Maurice says. I'll act grown-up and devote myself to art!"

"What did you say, dear?" Aunt Toosie asked, pushing my door open with her hip because in one hand she was carrying a tremendous glass of orange juice over crushed ice and in the other, a small glass chuck full of—milk of magnesia.

"I said, maybe it's my appendix!" I put my hand on my stomach. "Aunt Eveline used to say you're not supposed to take milk of magnesia if you have a stomachache."

Aunt Toosie paused. "You didn't say you had a stomachache!"

"Ah-de-la-eed! The truth, please!" I heard Aunt Eveline distinctly.

"My stomach's okay, Aunt Eveline, I've paid for my sins." I gulped down the milk of magnesia and put the orange juice on the table by my bed. "You don't have to call the doctor, Aunt Toosie. I have a cold because I went to bed with a wet head."

"Oh, dear, how foolish! But if you're positive that's it, we'll wait a bit to see how you do. Here are two aspirin with your juice, and try to go back to sleep." Aunt Toosie went to the window and closed the shutters. She patted my shoulder and said, "Rest now, dear," and tiptoed out.

I had too much on my mind to rest. Besides, I was afraid that if I fell asleep, I'd forget to breathe through my mouth, so I kept myself awake thinking of the future.

"Magnificent, Dolores dearest!" cried Louis, gazing at my landscape painting and the First Place blue ribbon pinned on it. "Dolores, my darling I can't stop thinking of you. Every moment of the day you are in my thoughts, driving me to distraction! Come away with me, my darling!"

"Oh, Louis," I said, "you're sweet, you really are, but I have my career to think about."

He looked so crushed I hurried on, "But wait a bit, Louis dear, until I've really established myself as an artist. It won't be long, I promise you that much." Modestly, I refrained from listing the other prizes I'd won for my paintings, sure indications that success was near. Nor did

I tell him that Leonard McClosky had also proposed and been told to wait.

I tossed my heavy black hair back and re-pinned it with the Spanish comb.

"My God, you're beautiful!" said Louis in an awed whisper.

"Kerr-choo!" My whole head felt the explosion. I blew my nose and went to the window to breathe. I opened the shutters and tried to take a deep breath. Just as I was turning around to go back to bed, I saw the shutter in my old room open. The girl next door stood in the window, separated from me by not more than the width of a room. It was hard to tell how old she was because she was so thin. Her arms were like bones covered with skin, and her head seemed too big for her scrawny neck. Her eyes were dark and enormous; her hair was as black as Dolores del Rio's and as curly as Sandra Lee's. We stared so long, I had to say something. I said, "Hello!" and then, "Hello, Norma Jean."

She smiled and her face came alive. As skinny as she was I could see she would have been pretty, a real Latin beauty, with a few—no, not a few, with many more—pounds.

"Hello, Addie," she answered. She knew my name too!

"How did you know my name!?"

"You knew mine," she said.

"Yes, but..." I'd forgotten how I'd learned her name, but it was in an ordinary way. Oh, yes, I remembered. The postman had told me.

"The new folks is named Valerie," he had said. "The little gal's name is Norma. Miss Norma Jean Valerie. Moved in from the country so the little gal can see a city doctor."

"The postman told me your name. I have a cold and I'm supposed to spend the day in bed. Are you sick too?"

"No, I'm not sick," was her surprising answer, "but they think so and I have to go to doctors all the time."

What cruel parents! No wonder she was so thin. It was uncomfortable standing in the window talking loud enough to hear each other but not loud enough to be heard by Aunt Toosie and Sandra Lee.

"I used to live in your room," I said, "and my cousin Sandra Lee lived in this one. One time when we weren't fighting we made a telegraph wire, at least that's what we called it, between our houses, you know. Tom showed me how." I had forgotten she didn't know Tom. "He lives on the other side of you," I added.

"I know," she said. "I saw him walking his dog this morning. He looks just like Louis." I wondered how she knew who Louis was and was about to ask when she added, "How do you make a telegraph wire?"

"Well, that's just a name for it, of course. It really is one big loop of string attached to each window. There's a clothespin at one end to clip your telegraphs and letters to and when the other person pulls her end of the string, the clothespin moves across like a pulley."

"That would be fun! Let's do it."

"It'll take me a while. I'll have to sneak out of my room to the kitchen for supplies."

"All right," said Norma Jean happily. "I'll be writing a letter to you while you make the telegraph wire." And without waiting to see what I'd answer, she left the window.

I tiptoed to my door and opened it a crack. Not a sound. Sandra Lee was in her room. I sneaked into the hall and creaked down the steps. On the tenth one, Sandra Lee said, "You're no more sick than I am." She was standing on the top step. When she saw my face, she added, "Your nose is red and fat! You look awful."

"Make up your mind," I said. "First you say I'm not sick, then you say I am."

"I didn't say you were sick. I said your nose looks ugly. You caught a cold last night going out on a school night, didn't you! I'll have to tell Mama so she'll know what you have and what to do to make you well."

Sandra Lee brushed past me on the steps calling, "Mama! Addie caught cold going out on a school night!" Give her rope to hang herself, I thought.

I came into the kitchen in time to hear Aunt Toosie say, "Addie told me all about it, Sandra Lee. Don't be a tattle-tale." It was a pleasure to smile sweetly at Sandra Lee.

"Hah! They've held 'em!" Uncle Henry's voice came from behind the newspaper.

"Who, Daddy? Who held who?" Sandra Lee asked excitedly, forgetting about me. I could tell she thought

Uncle Henry was reading about yesterday's game and was hoping Leonard's touchdown was mentioned.

"Whom," I said. "Who held whom."

"O.K., then, whom, Daddy?"

Uncle Henry lowered the newspaper and peered first at me, then at Sandra Lee. "Hitler is whom," he said. "And the Russians are who. They've stopped the Huns at Moscow! Does that interest you?"

"Oh, it does me, Uncle Henry," I lied. "What else is new?"

"Yeah, sure!" Sandra Lee said to me. "I just bet you care! So you can impress a certain older, married man with how much you know and how grown-up you are!"

"Girls!" shouted Aunt Toosie at the kitchen door. She'd caught the married man part and was looking at me in horror.

"Time to go to the office," Uncle Henry said, stumbling out of his chair in his hurry to escape.

"*Whom* were you discussing?" Aunt Toosie asked, her eyes glued to me.

"I've been discussing foreign events with Tom and Tom's father," I said hurriedly, before Sandra Lee had a chance.

"Goodbye, Toosie." Uncle Henry, hat in hand, looked in from the hall. "Sometimes, I think you girls don't know there's a world out there beyond Audubon Street!"

"Yes, we do, Daddy," Sandra Lee called to his retreating

back. "We talk about the war with our friends a lot."

Sandra Lee didn't mention that our discussions usually centered on things like how handsome some boy we knew would look in a Marine uniform.

"Then tell your friends that this country is asleep," called Uncle Henry, "and we're going to wake up with Hirohito in *California*!"

The front door slammed. Uncle Henry was like Tom and could get all worked up over the newspaper.

"Oh, look, Mama," said Sandra Lee. "Addie's walking barefooted with a cold!"

"Oh, Addie, darling, you shouldn't! What do you want, dear?"

"I came to get a glass of warm water and salt to gargle with," I said.

"Please, Addie, go back to bed. Sandra Lee will bring it up, won't you dear?"

"No, I won't, I'm late for school," said Dear rudely. "It's her own fault she's sick and she can get her own salt water."

"Sandra Lee! Come back here! You're not supposed to talk to anyone like that. You…"

And while Aunt Toosie chased after Sandra Lee to the front of the house and onto the porch, I found my string, a clothespin, a heavy spoon with a hole at the top of the handle, and two oatmeal cookies. I went upstairs and glanced out the window before closing my shutters. I couldn't see Norma Jean and I heard Aunt Toosie coming upstairs. I found my pink, rabbit-fur slippers and hurried to the bathroom. I made gargling noises and poured the hot, salt water down the washbasin.

"That's better," I said, coming out of the bathroom at the same time Aunt Toosie came into my room. "I think I can rest now, Aunt Toosie."

"Good, dear. Sandra Lee apologizes. She's very, very sorry she was rude." Aunt Toosie went through the tucking-me-in process again. "I'll bring you some more fruit juice later on," she said.

As soon as she'd left I opened my shutters but there was still no sign of Norma Jean Valerie. I didn't dare call. I spent the whole morning checking her window and plodding through a theme Sister Maurice had assigned about an imaginary conversation with God.

"Use lively dialogue," she'd said, "and *vivid* description! You are *there*!"

I had just finished in pencil and was about to copy it in ink when Aunt Toosie came in with fruit juice and began reading aloud over my shoulder.

"'A Celestial Conversation,'" she said, happily. "That's a nice title." I hate people to read my themes aloud. I slunk down under my sheets and listened to my words:

"Alone on a small cloud, I floated forward and faced God.

'Ah-de-lade!' said God. 'I see by your record that you have sinned exceedingly in Thought, Word, and Deed!'

'Oh, yes, Your Majesty,' I answered politely. 'I confess that I have gone and broken at least eight of the ten commandments, in fact, maybe all of them, but I'm not sure about adultery and coveting my neighbor's wife because, you see, I am not married yet and besides I am a girl but maybe to be perfectly honest I should substitute husband and it's true I have been noticing a certain, *possibly* married man, so maybe that might come under the same heading as the coveting wife or the adultery ones, it's up to you, God, and that about covers it unless I've forgotten anything, and you are welcome to add it to the list!'"

Aunt Toosie's voice was getting shaky but she continued.

"'Ah-de-lade! Are you truly sorry for your sins?'

'Oh, yes, Your Majesty, I am hardily sorry for having offended Thee. Through my fault, through my fault, through my most grievous fault!'

'All right, then, Adelaide, you'll have to spend a short time in Purgatory, that's a place not quite as hot as Hell, but after that you may live in Heaven with your dear mother, Darling Pasie, and your Aunt Eveline at 16B St. Peter Avenue, a very good address, with an excellent view of earth from the living room window.'

'Oh thank you, Your Majesty!' I said, floating happily backwards to the other clouds.

The End."

"Addie!" Aunt Toosie moaned and sank into a chair. "You don't believe—you don't believe it really is… that God really is like that, do you?"

I modified my answer. "Sort of," I said.

"Addie, God is *Love!*"

I said a silent prayer of thanks that Aunt Toosie did not know I knew all about real love from *Dearest.*

"And—and the married man?" she continued. "I hardly dare ask—but that's just fiction, of course, isn't it? I mean you made it up, of course?"

"Oh sure! Don't worry about it, Aunt Toosie," I lied. "It's not in ink yet and I have till Monday."

"Oh, God," said Aunt Toosie, who never used the name of the Lord in vain. "I am going to give you catechism lessons every afternoon until we clear this up."

I stifled a groan and tried to smile sweetly. Maybe she would forget quicker if I didn't make a big thing over it. "Thank you, Aunt Toosie," I said, watching her tear up "The Celestial Conversation" into very small pieces and drop them into my wastebasket.

"Your first lesson is: God is Love! Write your theme for Sister Maurice with that title. Oh, God," she said again and then murmured, "what would Eveline do?" She left my room, forgetting to take the empty glass.

The last thing I wanted to do was rewrite my theme. I hate themes. Come to think of it, I was sick to death of school. The only thing I cared about was art class, and I already knew more than the teacher because Aunt Eveline had taught me so much.

By the time I'd written "God is Love" and nibbled at the baked potato on my lunch tray, I'd given up on Norma Jean and was bored with the whole world. I didn't care if she ever came to the window. I didn't even care if I never became an artist. And I certainly did not care about Louis, Leonard, or Tom, in that order. My head hurt worse, my nose was still stopped up, and my throat was so sore I could hardly swallow, much less talk. I spent the afternoon dozing and waking, and by four, Dr. Chapman appeared over my bed and proceeded to thump my chest and take my blood pressure.

Writing on his prescription pad, he said to Aunt Toosie, "Bronchitis. You'll have to keep her in bed, and I'll be back Friday to see her. Call me if you need me before then."

That sounded ominous. Why would Aunt Toosie need him unless I was worse, and how could I get any worse without dying? I groaned, and Dr. Chapman patted my hand, "I know you're uncomfortable, Addie, but this prescription will help you. Stay in bed, you hear?"

"Um," I said and groaned again.

"Poor darling," murmured Aunt Toosie as they were leaving my room.

"Did Tom call?" I croaked.

"No, dear," she said. "He has no way of knowing you're ill, and I saw him leave the house early. He's trying to get Jesuit to take him back in mid-semester. Rest now, dear."

Rest?! How could I rest when my love life had ended before it had even begun? Louis probably thought it was my fault Tom hated him, and Tom didn't even realize I'd caught a cold on his account. How could I ever become a famous artist if my personal love life was in such a mess?

Four

Dr. Chapman's medicine, which tasted first like peppermint and then eased into bitter almond, worked, and my nose opened enough to let me breathe and sleep through the night. The next morning when Aunt Toosie appeared with orange juice I was all dried up; my head was still heavy, but I knew I'd live. She felt my brow and said, "Much better," and hurried out of my room to fix breakfast, "Don't get out of bed for anything, Addie!"

The minute she left, I heard something hit the screen. I went to the window and saw Norma Jean. She'd taken the screen out of her window.

"I threw an eraser," she said. "Can you fix the telegraph line now?" She was waving an envelope. "I've written you a letter."

"It must be the story of your life; it took you so long."

"It is," she replied. "I'm telling you everything."

"Oh!" That sounded interesting. "I'll tie this spoon to a string and throw it to you." I throw well, because Tom taught me how to handle a football before he knew girls were supposed to act like ladies. Norma Jean caught the spoon on the first try. "Now you measure off a long-enough piece and throw the spoon back to me. Hang on to your end!"

Norma Jean took two throws, and I almost fell out of the window catching the spoon on the second try. I clipped the clothespin on where the spoon had been and tied the ends of the string so that there was a big loop between our windows. Then I pulled one end while Norma Jean watched the clothespin working its way back to her. She was smiling so happily it almost made up for the dark rings under her eyes.

"There you are," she cried, clipping the envelope to the clothespin and sending it over to me.

I was afraid the clothespin wouldn't hold her heavy letter. "All right," I said, "tie your end to your window for next time and put the screen back. I'll send you a message this afternoon."

I was just replacing my screen when I heard her cry out and looked across in time to see my old screen falling to the ground.

"I dropped it!" she cried. "They'll be furious!"

She let go the string and disappeared from the window. I gathered up the whole telegraph line and put it in my drawer, hoping sincerely that if Norma Jean's parents were that mean, her screen would never be connected to me. With a slightly guilty conscience, I got back in bed and opened the pink envelope. There were ten sheets of pink scented stationary; N.J.V. was engraved in graceful darker pink at the top of each sheet. Norma Jean's first sentence was: "My name is Norma Jean Valerie and I hate the woman married to my father." Was she serious? Did she mean her mother? Or—I heard someone coming. Sandra Lee was coming upstairs with my breakfast tray. I hid the letter.

"Breakfast is served, Madame," Sandra Lee said, kicking open my door. Something was making her happy and it certainly wasn't waiting on me.

"Louis is driving me to school this morning," she said, "and, I had a long talk with Tom yesterday." She smiled in a mean way and watched me for a reaction.

"Well," I said, "maybe you'd like my cold so you could have everything that belongs to me."

"I'm not going to catch your old cold." She plunked the tray in my lap, sloshing the café au lait, and hurried as fast as she could back to my door. "Louis says they should have called me Guinevere." She tossed her heavy golden curls. "She's King Arthur's wife, you know. She was a beautiful blond."

"Yes, and she was false! False to King Arthur. She seduced Lancelot, who was pure. Guinevere is a good name for you, all right. Anyhow, Louis thinks I look like Dolores del Rio!"

"Dolores del Rio?! What a joke!" said Sandra Lee happily. "You're just jealous, and you're stuck there with your red nose. Tom asked me to wait for him after football practice this afternoon." She slammed my door and called,

"Bye, bye, Dolores!"

I could hear her light footsteps down the hall taking her out to the happy day that lay ahead. I looked at the pink letter under my sheet. Suddenly, I didn't care if Norma Jean hated her mother. I didn't care about anything except the tragic story of Adelaide Aspasie Agnew, stricken in her prime just at the moment when life might have been beautiful. I pushed my tray aside and cried until my nose was all stopped up again. I got out of bed to throw cold water on my face, and when I got back in, I nibbled on some toast with jam and, for want of something better to do, started reading Norma Jean's letter again.

"I am the daughter of Simeon Valerie, a planter, and I grew up at Oakwood Plantation on the Mississippi River.

"My mother died when I was a baby and I was brought up by my father."

I was so deep into Norma Jean's letter, I didn't even notice someone was standing at my door. He must have knocked, but it wasn't until he said, "Addie, may I come in?" that I saw Tom's Uncle Malvern holding a bunch of gardenias.

"Your mother's favorite flowers," Uncle Malvern said. "Heard you were sick. They don't smell too heavy, do they? The gardenias, I mean?" It was typical of my powers over the opposite sex that my very first flowers were from Uncle Malvern instead of Louis or even Tom.

"They don't smell at all as far as I'm concerned," I said.

"My nose is stopped up."

"Of course! How stupid of me. I didn't want to disturb you. I'll just leave these with Toosie and wish you a speedy recovery."

He had almost shut the door when I realized how rude I was being. "Uncle Malvern! Don't go! I mean, come in, please. Don't come too close because of my cold, but can't you stay a minute?" He looked pleased, so I added, "I'm bored silly here by myself and I wish you'd stay. How—how is Louis? And—and Tom?"

"I'll just stay a minute, Addie, and I'll sit right here by the window. Louis and Tom are just fine. I thought you might like to hear the neighborhood gossip!" Uncle Malvern giggled, and I wondered for the millionth time what my mother had seen in him that made her love him more than anyone, including my father.

"Yes, what's been happening?" I asked, trying to work some enthusiasm into my question.

"Well, of course, you haven't been out of commission long, but something interesting did happen this morning. I was in the garden picking these flowers for you, and I heard a noise that sounded like something big had fallen. I ran next door and discovered the screen to your old window lying on the ground. So I picked it up and carried it to the Valerie's front door and knocked. I got the master of the house, Mr. Simeon Valerie himself, a funny looking, dark-haired fellow with big bushy eyebrows and a moustache like Teddy Roosevelt. I seem to remember him from somewhere....but never mind. He didn't know me, that's for sure. 'Good morning, sir!' I said as cheerfully as possible. 'I'm your neighbor and I just heard a screen fall out your window. Thought you'd like to have it back!' 'Put it there,' he said, pointing to the porch floor, and then as an afterthought he added, 'Thanks', and shut the door. Imagine not even asking my name! A queer fellow! And his bride—they haven't been married long, you know! And you'll never guess who the new Mrs. Valerie is!" Uncle Malvern added in a gossipy way. My head was reeling.

"A famous movie star?" I asked.

"Ha-ha, hee-hee," Uncle Malvern giggled. "I'll tell you a secret. I overheard Louis talking to her—Eliza, she's called. Yes indeedy, she's an acquaintance of his, and it's my thought that Louis' return and Eliza's arrival at Three Twenty Audubon Street are not purely coincidental, if you get my meaning."

I could only stare at Uncle Malvern. He was silly all right, but—I realized my finger hurt because I had twisted a corner of my sheet into a tight rope and was winding it around like a tourniquet. Did he mean Louis liked Eliza? That made a definite triangle—unless you counted Aunt Mabel. Was there such a thing as a rectangle? Why had Louis acted in the car as though he didn't even know Eliza? I tried to remember exactly what he'd said.

"Tom looks great, doesn't he?" Once Uncle Malvern

starts talking, he's hard to stop." I showed him The Machine last night, and you know what he said?"

"What?" I was trying to sound interested, but I was in shock over Louis and Eliza.

"He said it reminded him of Jules Verne's Time Machine! Now that's a compliment, isn't it? And I began to think of how much I'd like to go back in time, see things that took place long ago."

"Yes," I said.

"It would be nice to go back and live on a plantation," Uncle Malvern said dreamily.

"Provided, of course, you weren't one of the slaves," I said, "or a young man about to get killed in the Civil War." Was he ever going to leave?

"Oh, well, of course. But I was thinking of the old romantic South," Uncle Malvern said. "It's fiction, of course, Jules Verne's Time Machine, but he's written lots of fiction about inventions of the future that came true—like the submarine. Well, Addie, Tom's too kind to pull my leg, and he might not really believe I could do such a thing—I mean he might just have made the comparison to show an interest and be friendly—but the truth is the idea's caught my fancy. I've worked on the Perpetual Motion Machine long enough; why not give the Time Machine a try?"

Uncle Malvern looked as though he'd forgotten where he was. "A plantation," he repeated. "Louis mentioned the Valerie plantation. Well, now, I'll be going—shouldn't have stayed so long! By the way, my dear, I have a feeling you figure in the schemes of our friend in the Salvation Army! Get well soon!"

"What schemes?" I asked, but Uncle Malvern just smiled in a silly way, waved from my door, and shut it. Could he possibly mean romantic schemes, and that I was competition for a grown-up woman? Maybe she was after Louis more than he was after her. Maybe she wasn't pretty. I picked up Norma Jean's letter again, hoping there might be some clue about Eliza and Louis in it.

When I was little, (the letter continued) *my nurse used to say "Sugar Pie, you always was the prettiest baby I ever saw, with your black curls and honey-colored skin! Eat your sweet potatoes and rice, and put a little meat on those bones, and all the young gentlemen in Louisiana'll be at your feet!" But I didn't care about young gentlemen at my feet. If my father was pleased with me, that was enough.*

In the evening when my father rode in from the fields, I'd watch him gallop across the lawn, silhouetted against the sunset. "How's my girl?" my father'd say as he swung out of the saddle and came to me. "My, doesn't she look pretty! A real young lady!" After he'd bathed and dressed, we'd go in to dinner together, and he'd treat me like the lady of the house.

But if we had guests, I wasn't allowed to eat with

them. I'd sit upstairs in my room listening to the deep voices of the men and the silvery laughter of the ladies. There was one woman who was already there. Eliza. She taught school in town. She was tall and slender and held her head as though she were balancing a crown on top of her blond hair. The first time she came to our house, she said to me, "You're pretty as a picture, my dear. When you lose your baby fat, you'll be the belle of the parish!" I turned red with shame. My father said, "Oh, come now, Eliza, she's not fat, she's just pleasingly plump!" He laughed and turned his back to me. I was so humiliated I ran upstairs and cried myself to sleep, and vowed I'd never in my whole life eat another thing.

A few weeks later, we were at dinner, my father and I, and he said, "Norma Jean, why aren't you eating the flan?"

"I'm not really interested in cup custard," I said.

He laughed. "Aha! There must be a young gentleman in your life! You're watching your figure!"

I fought tears. "Oh, Daddy," I said, "you're the only gentleman in my life!"

"That's very sweet of you, Sugar-Pie," he said seriously. "You've always been a sweet child, and I know you're going to be nice to Eliza when she comes to live with us. We're getting married, Norma Jean, isn't that wonderful? You'll have a mother again."

Just like that, he told me. I made myself get up and

go over and kiss him. "That's wonderful, Papa," I said, choking on the words.

After their marriage everything changed. My father was so busy trying to please her, he didn't have time for me anymore.

Then one night I heard Eliza and my father fighting in their bedroom, and I heard her shouting something about me.

"Norma Jean doesn't need medical help," my father answered quietly.

"That's true if you mean that old country bumble-foot of a doctor, but she does need a capable physician," said my stepmother, "and a little less of that Miss Sugar-Pie stuff. Tell her she has to eat. We ought to take her to New Orleans and get some decent medical help. Just for a while. I know of a house for rent."

The very next day, we packed up and came into town. We stayed at a hotel for a week until we moved here. Oh, Addie, I hate it. I want to go back to Oakwood. Please be my friend and help me get rid of Eliza so things will be the way they used to be!

I jumped out of bed and ran to the window. Norma Jean's screen was back in place and her shutters were closed.

"Norma Jean!" I yelled, scratching my throat.

There was no answer from Three Twenty Audubon Street.

It all fit: Uncle Malvern had said it wasn't a coincidence that Eliza and Louis had arrived in New Orleans at the same time. Eliza had talked Mr. Valerie into moving so that she could be near Louis.

Five

I spent two more boring days in bed. No one came to see me, and Norma Jean's window stayed shuttered. Maybe Norma Jean was gagged and tied to her bed by her wicked stepmother who wanted to run away with Louis.

I tried to imagine what Eliza looked like. "Tall and slender," Norma Jean had written. Maybe that meant skinny without curves. I could hope, anyway. I tried drawing self-portraits as Aunt Eveline had taught me, just to make the time pass, but my reflection in the mirror was too discouraging and my drawings too realistic.

Aunt Toosie went by Aunt Eveline's health rules: one fever-free day in bed, another in the house with frequent rests, and, finally, "limited activity" outside. If that third day fell during the week, the limited activity was half a day at school.

I was on my way back from school for lunch on the third day when I saw Tom running Pumpkin. I wasn't about to speak to him after the way he'd ignored me. I started across the street.

Brakes screeched.

"Jeez-us, Addie, you almost walked in front of that car!"

Tom yelled, grabbing me by the arm and yanking me to the curb. "Are you blind or something?"

"Can't you open your mouth without taking the Lord's name in vain?!" I felt weak in the knees at my narrow escape. "I'm not blind, I—I was thinking about a passage from the Bible." It wasn't a complete lie. "Sister Maurice read my composition to the class. It was about Love." Tom wasn't listening to what I was saying.

"You can't daydream like that!" he said. "You have to look where you're going. You almost—Addie, I'm sorry I gave you a hard time the other night. Are you mad at me?"

"No," I said. I have to admit the way Tom can apologize is very nice. *Dearest* was full of ideas about how to get a man to say he was sorry, but you didn't have to use them with Tom.

"I was walking Pumpkin. She needs some exercise, for a change," Tom added just as I was thinking how nice he was.

"That's a dirty dig if ever I heard one," I said. "I exercised Pumpkin lots while you were gone, but I've been sick lately, in case you haven't noticed."

"I noticed."

"When are you going to start back to school?"

"Mom talked to the principal and I start back tomorrow. They'll give me credit for the first part of the semester. I've been working out at practice, and they need me on the football team."

"They do need you, Tom," I said. "They need all the help

they can get."

"Thanks, Addie!" he said.

It was just like Tom to take that for a compliment, and I noticed he said my name in an ordinary way. Not Addie, like Leonard. "Why aren't you going back to school in North Carolina?" I asked.

"My mother needs me. I'm going to practice later this afternoon. I may play in Saturday's game."

It was too bad Tom wasn't a little more sophisticated. He had covered football and Pumpkin, and I was waiting for him to start on his third topic, Hitler, but he said. "By then I hope he's gone, but he says he'll stay until he puts his house in order! He thinks he can just walk in, make a few flowery speeches, and it'll make up for ten years. I asked him what he'd been doing all that time—he's supposed to be a geologist, but my mother says he's never done a lick of work. Anyhow, you know what he said? He said, 'I've been searching, Tom. I was searching, trying to find a meaning to my life!' So I asked him if he'd found anything and he said, 'I found the answer was and still is hidden right here at home. I've walked in a circle!' I guess after all that he expected me to say something like 'Isn't that wonderful?', but it made me so mad, I just walked out."

"Oh, Tom, you shouldn't have done that!" I noticed he hadn't called his father by name during the whole speech. "I know what your father did is awful," I said, "but he's really sorry now."

"Sorry?! What good does that do?!" Tom was getting madder, and Pumpkin was bored with the sidewalk and pulling at his leash.

"Well, if you won't forgive him, it doesn't do any good. Why don't you Forgive and Forget!" I'd read that phrase in Chapter II, called "Making up and Making over."

"You try it," Tom said. "Try forgiving Sandra Lee for all the things you're always complaining about."

"That's different," I said.

Just as I was about to tell Tom off, Aunt Mabel came out of Aunt Toosie's and waved.

"Hello, there, Addie," she said cheerfully. "How do you feel? Isn't it wonderful Tom's come home to stay?" She gave Tom such a loving look, it made her soft and pretty, and I wondered why she didn't use that look on Louis. "Come have lunch with us, Addie. Toosie gave me enough red beans to feed an army—even part of the Salvation Army." Aunt Mabel's expression changed, and she laughed the way you do when something's not funny.

If Aunt Mabel was unhappy when we all sat down to lunch, she did a good job of covering it up. She had something to say to everyone: Uncle Malvern, Tom, and me—everyone except Louis. She talked in an animated way, as though she were divinely happy and Louis wasn't there. I noticed she had done nothing to her hair, and it was pulled back into a French twist so tight it looked like some kind of self-torture.

"Well, now, here we are. Isn't this nice?" said Aunt Mabel. "I don't know about you, but I'm starved! I'll bet you are too, Tom! And, Addie, you need to eat to get strong again…" and on and on.

It must have been catching, because pretty soon I was blabbing away, too, afraid that if I didn't talk, Louis and Tom would fight. I heard myself telling everyone about the two upcoming, thrilling events of my life, the Christmas pageant at school and the dreaded Fall dance, as though I were looking forward to them both. In the middle of one of my speeches, the kitchen door opened, and there stood Nini with a bowl of fluffy white rice in her hands.

I hadn't seen her in months and was hoping she'd say something like, "Look at that young lady! Isn't she grown-up and lovely!" Instead, she said, "Well, look at my little girl!"

I stopped myself from jumping up and hugging her like I wanted to. In grown-up, ladylike tones I said, "Good day, Nini. I hope you are feeling well?" and, unable to resist myself, added, "How's Holly?"

Nini said, beaming on me as though I were five years old, "Growing up fast, just like you. We'll do some talking after lunch, Addie, honey," she added, as she circled the table with the rice.

"Now, isn't that nice?" Aunt Mabel said. "Nini's here 'pinch-hitting' for me a few days."

"Tell us about the Salvation Army," Uncle Malvern

said to Louis. "What do they do besides stand around with tin cups and sing?"

I thought that was a mean thing for Uncle Malvern to say, but Louis answered as he helped himself to the rice Nini held. "The Army helps people who are down and out. You'd be surprised at how many people there are now who are just plain hungry—starving, really; they have no hope left, and to lose hope is to lose your life unless someone helps you."

"It's called despair, Louis," Aunt Mabel said coldly. "It's a sin in the Catholic Church."

It seemed to me she had missed the point, and the boat as well. Louis looked like she'd slapped him.

"I remember that, Mabel," he answered. "There's very little I've forgotten."

Aunt Mabel blushed and said, "Tell us more about the Salvation Army."

"They have a house. I'm talking about New York City— and if you're destitute you can go there and have a bed and meals. They never preach at you; they just take care of you and make you feel wanted. Knowing someone cares is more powerful than all the words that could be said."

"Amen to that," said Aunt Mabel, and it was Louis' turn to blush.

I noticed he had not mentioned anything personal about what he had done at the Salvation Army; it was as though he was giving a lecture explaining what the Army did. I tried to figure out how Tom was taking it, but he seemed to be concentrating on the design of his plate, and all I could see was his straw blond hair covering his eyes.

"Louis," I said, wondering if I should call him Uncle Louis, "have you seen Three Twenty Audubon Street on the inside yet?"

Tom looked up, frowned at me, and mouthed, "Shut up!"

As I said this, Nini came back into the room to pass the red beans. I could tell she was listening extra hard to what we were saying. I tried to catch her eye, but she was all business, as though the red beans would jump out of the dish unless she kept her eyes glued to them.

"Why yes!" said Louis. "How do you like those new people, Tom?"

"They're O.K.," Tom said.

"And the young lady in the family?" Louis continued cheerfully.

"She's O.K.," said Tom sullenly.

I knew from experience that Louis ought to give up, but he continued, and he was still acting as though he didn't know the Valeries well.

"May I be excused, Mom?" Tom said. "I have practice this afternoon."

"Don't you want a bit more, dear?" Aunt Mabel asked. It was as though Louis wasn't there.

"No, thank you." Tom was already standing up.

"Addie hasn't finished yet, Tom," Louis said. "Sit down."

Tom turned to Louis. "I asked my mother," he said. "This is not your house and you have nothing to say about what I do."

"You could show me some respect, young man," said Louis. "In spite of everything, I'm still your father."

"Oh, God!" said Tom.

"Oh, dear!" Aunt Mabel said, biting her lip. Her eyes were brim-full, and her nose was getting pink.

"If I've got to sit here," said Tom angrily, "I'd like to know what was so important that you had to leave—desert—my mother."

"Nothing was that important. I made a terrible mistake," Louis said earnestly.

"And you think being sorry will make up for all those years?" whined Aunt Mabel.

"How else can he make up for them?" I said those words! I certainly hadn't meant to speak out loud; it just tumbled out. "I—I'm sorry," I said. Everyone was staring at me. "I beg your pardon! Of course, it's none of my business."

"No, no, wait, Addie," said Louis. "I want to hear what you think. You're an outside observer."

Tom was looking at me. His eyes were hard. I was on the spot, having, as usual, put myself there.

"I—I don't mean that it wasn't a terrible thing to do, leave your little baby and your wife. But if you're sorry, really sorry, and want to make it up, how else can you, if they won't forgive you to begin with?"

"There!" said Louis triumphantly. "That's what I'm trying to say, said by an impartial observer. All I'm asking for is a second chance. Will you give it to me, Mabel?"

Aunt Mabel's tears had disappeared without falling, and her face was set in unforgiving lines. "You may stay through Christmas, Louis," she said, ice hanging on every word. Something had gone out of Aunt Mabel during all those years; I didn't need to read *Dearest* to know that. I looked at Tom, and just for a second, I caught a vulnerable look on his face. Louis had a second chance with him. The only trouble was, Louis didn't know how to go about it. He didn't know Tom as well as I did.

"Thank you, Mabel," Louis said quietly. "And thank you, Addie," he said gratefully. I felt my face turn red.

"Don't bother to thank me," Tom said, getting up and slamming his napkin on the table without folding it. "I have to go to practice." He left without looking at me.

"Well, Mabel," Louis said, "I haven't gotten very far with that young man, but I haven't given up. I'd like some more of your delicious salad, if you don't mind. Addie, Mr. Valerie asked me to come by. Maybe you and I could pay a short visit to Three Twenty after lunch?"

"I'd love to visit Three Twenty!" I said, taken by surprise.

There was a shattering crash. Nini had dropped Aunt Mabel's crystal water pitcher on the polished floor, and cubes of ice and splintered crystal lay indistinguishable in the ice water. Everyone jumped up to help even though the situation needed only one person with a mop. That person was standing stock still staring at me. She turned to the kitchen for the mop and I followed.

"Ain't you shamed making sweet eyes at that old man?" she said after I'd caught up with her. "You stay away from him *and* Three Twenty. Don't do no good back-tracking." Nini hadn't paused in her journey to the broom closet. "Don't stir up no ghosts."

"That's not why you don't want me there!" I cried, grabbing the mop handle ahead of her and trying to make her look at me.

"Get out my way and let me clean that mess," she said.

By then, Aunt Mabel was with us and Nini said to her, "I'm broken up like that pitcher! I don't know how I come to break that lovely old pitcher!"

"Don't you worry, Nini," Aunt Mabel said. "It was a wedding present and my marriage is smashed too—far worse than the pitcher." Aunt Mabel's voice wobbled.

"No need to be nice to me," Nini said. "I deserves a set back for being clumsy but Addie's Aunt gave me a pitcher once and now it's yours. I'm putting your name on it. I'll bring it next time I come."

"Why, thank you, Nini!" said Aunt Mabel. "I'd rather have a pitcher from you than—than one that symbolizes—that stands for the biggest mistake I ever made!" And with that, Aunt Mabel burst into tears just as Louis came into the kitchen.

It was all so awkward, I just stood there like a dumbbell while Nini put her arm around Aunt Mabel and Louis said quietly to me, "I think it's a good time for us to go next door, Addie."

"Yes. Oh yes," I said stumbling over the broom in a hurry to follow Louis. I wasn't out the door before Nini's words made me stop and turn around.

"Adelaide," she said in a commanding voice, "you go poking around and you're sure to stir up mischief! I know you, Adelaide Aspasie Agnew, and I'm speaking for your Aunt Eveline when I saw you wasn't among those invited, so you got no business horning in."

"Listen, Nini," I said, "It's you that's minding other people's business. You've got no right telling me what to do. Not any more, you don't. I'm no baby and I'll do as I please." With that I marched out—not quite quickly enough.

"Miss Butinsky, sticking her big nose into everything!" she cried after me. She'd chosen her words carefully for maximum meanness.

"Louis! Louis!" I called. "I'm coming!" I caught up with him on the sidewalk. He'd had his feelings hurt too.

"Seems like the harder I try, the worse I do, Addie. Tom and Mabel will never forgive me. Even Malvern is on their side." He slowed his pace. "How about you, Addie? You like me, don't you?"

He was looking at me waiting for an answer. I waited so long trying to remember what I was supposed to answer according to *Dearest* that he repeated, "Don't you?" Caution to the winds, I whispered passionately, "Yes!" and lowered my eyes. It was not the most romantic place in the world, standing there in front of Tom's house, one foot in Aunt Mabel's nasturtiums, and I know Aunt Eveline was speechless with horror, but I was hoping to hear something like:

"Dolores, dearest girl, you are the one I've been searching for all these years. I've walked full circle and find my happiness here at home. Just say you love me a little, and I'll wait for you to grow up—for the rest of my life if necessary!"

"You should join the Army, Addie!" said Louis cheerfully. "You are just the kind of girl they need!" I looked up quickly, trying to pretend I'd only looked down at a nasturtium. "Love is what it's all about," Louis continued. "If you can't forgive and love your fellow man as you do, you save poor souls like me who need that."

It occurred to me that I wasn't the one Louis had wronged and so had nothing to forgive, but I was so relieved he hadn't noticed I was expecting something more personal, I sighed and tried to smile like one of the Salvation Army ladies with bonnets on the back of their heads.

"I love to help others," I said piously. Aunt Eveline's call was now ringing furiously in my ears, but I was busy marching next to Louis, pretending I was part of his Army, and tuned her out.

As we turned up the walk to Three Twenty, it was such a familiar thing to do, I felt as though I were stepping into the past; Aunt Eveline was waiting for me inside. Nini had probably made gumbo; I could almost smell the spicy seafood and burnt roux. I stopped walking, trying to conjure up the living room. I could see each piece of furniture and I knew the quality of the light filtering through the closed shutter, making bands where tiny particles of dust drifted. Suddenly, I thought, What am I doing? After I see the inside of Three Twenty changed, I will never again be able to imagine it as it was.

"I don't think I'll go in," I said to Louis in a panic.

"Oh, come on, now Addie!" he said. "They'll be delighted to see you."

It was too late to get out of it. As Louis rang the doorbell, I put one foot on the step and closed my eyes, hurrying in my mind through the upstairs hall for a last look at my old room. I saw the brass bed with shiny knobs, the patchwork quilt Aunt Eveline had made me, and the pine chest of drawers she'd said my father had made himself out of Honduran wood just for me. On the floor was the rug Aunt Eveline had braided, and hanging on the wall her watercolor of the lagoon at Audubon Park.

"Hello there," Mr. Valerie said as I opened my eyes. He was shaking hands with Louis. "Come in! Come in!" He hadn't noticed me.

"Here's Addie," said Louis turning to me, "your

neighbor on the other side."

Naturally, I tripped going up the steps. "How do you do?" I asked stupidly, picking myself up.

"I'm glad to see you, Addie," said Mr. Valerie. "I have a daughter just about your age, I'd guess, but she's not here at the moment. Come this way, you two," and I was once again inside Three Twenty.

Six

The living room was full of light and color, completely opposite to my memory of it. The furniture was all angles and blond wood instead of curlicues of mahogany, draped with linen slip covers in summer and grass rugs in place of wool ones; I would have no trouble keeping what seemed like two different places separate and clear in my mind.

Mr. Valerie wasn't what I'd expected either: I liked his bushy eyebrows and Teddy Roosevelt moustache and his curly black hair. He would have looked wonderful in a white linen suit and a wide-brimmed Panama hat, the kind planters are supposed to wear. I could just imagine him on a white horse, galloping across the land to Norma Jean waiting beneath the columns of Oakwood Plantation. When Eliza walked in, my heart sank. She was what *Dearest* called "a stunner" or a "knockout," with curves in the right places and a dress straight out of Vogue. I could see by the look in Mr. Valerie's face that he adored her, and I stole a glance at Louis to see what he thought, but his back was turned.

"Norma Jean will be happy to meet you as soon as she gets back from the hospital. She's just there for a few little tests," Eliza said in elegant, lady-like tones. If I lived to be a hundred I'd never learn to be that sophisticated. "Do you go to Our Lady's school?"

"Yes," I said feeling awkward and shy.

"Addie was telling us at lunch about a play Our Lady is putting on," said Louis. "It's called 'The Star of Bethlehem.' Isn't that right, Addie?"

"Uh-huh," I said. I am a great conversationalist.

"Isn't that nice," said Eliza in her cool tones. Her hair was silver-blond, a color that could only come from a bottle. With her ice-maiden good looks, she was perfectly cast as "the other woman" and/or the wicked stepmother. "Maybe there'll be a part for Norma Jean," Eliza added.

"Oh, they always need angels for the heavenly choir," I said. "Can she sing?"

"Like an angel." Mr. Valerie laughed at his joke. "And if you need an angel costume, there's one in the attic. As a matter of fact, there seems to be a costume for every occasion in a huge old armoire that belonged to your family, I understand."

"Oh, yes! I remember! We used to call it the Great Catch-all because it was where Aunt Eveline stored everything she couldn't find a place for—all the Mardi Gras costumes and broken toys that needed mending. Oh, I remember it well!"

"The armoire was too large to come down the steps, the Smiths told us, and your Aunt Toosie was supposed to clean it out but never did," Eliza said in accusing tones.

"What else is in the Great Catch-all besides costumes and broken toys?" Louis asked.

"All kinds of things," I answered. "Everything not used but too good to throw away, and anything that got broken. Aunt Eveline put it all in the Great Catch-all to decide about when spring cleaning came along."

"Hmm," said Louis. "I'll be glad to help you sort things out, Addie," he said, "and look for costumes for the play."

"Thank you," I said. I was dying to go through the Great Catch-all with Louis, and he was smiling at me as though he was looking forward to it, too. He was the only grown-up I'd ever known who treated me as an equal.

"I think Norma Jean lives in your old room upstairs, Addie," said Mr. Valerie, "the one at the end of the hall. Why don't you show her, Eliza?" I held my breath for fear she'd say no.

Eliza didn't look too pleased, but she stood up and led the way.

The Addie who'd lived in this house had been a little girl, playing paper dolls and dreaming about love. Now, I was in the middle of a real love affair with a married man. I couldn't cling to my childish memories, but I couldn't help wanting to see my old room. Meekly, I followed Eliza.

I had a moment's panic going upstairs as the second-to-last step squeaked just as it always had, even though the steps were carpeted in a fuzzy rug that covered the wood we had worn concave.

The hall upstairs was papered in a leafy pattern that made you feel you were walking along the tops of trees. It was all so different, the memories of my family seemed erased, until I passed the attic door and caught a whiff of cedar. I had the silly feeling that my family ghosts were stored in the attic, neatly layered in tissue paper inside our old cedar chests.

I hurried as Eliza motioned me ahead of her into my old room.

Except for organdy curtains and a mahogany bed with a ruffled organdy tester, my room was exactly as I remembered. There was the glass-topped porch door and an old pine chest, almost the twin of the one my father had made. The rug was woven instead of braided, but the colors were the same as mine. There was a painting on the wall exactly where I'd hung Aunt Eveline's watercolor, except that this was a painting of a plantation house, its white columns gleaming behind moss-draped oak trees.

My room even smelled the same—a mixture of Aunt Eveline's jasmine vine and the very faintest hint of cloves from an old, long discarded potpourri.

"Does it upset you, seeing your old room? Is it very different?" Eliza asked.

"It's the same," I said with a deep sigh. "All of it. It looks just like it did before, except I had a brass bed with a quilt."

"Oh, that bed is in the attic! I remember the Smiths

saying they'd gotten it from your family because 'the little girl wanted a new bed when she moved.' We put it in the attic because Norma Jean insisted on having *her* bed brought all the way from the country." Eliza said this in a disgusted way.

"I wish I'd kept my old bed," I said. "Aunt Toosie told me I could fix up my room at her house exactly as I wanted, and I chose everything new and Early American."

Eliza laughed for the first time. Pretty dimples showed in her cheeks. "Your old brass bed is really Early American," she said. "I love it too, but, well Norma Jean—she's not really my daughter, you know, and she didn't have a mother for so long, and when I married her father, she—she couldn't forgive him—or me. Whatever I like she hates—except her father." Eliza walked out of the room. "Are you ready?" she asked.

I couldn't help feeling a little sorry for Eliza, because she knew Norma Jean hated her. I took a last look around my old room and followed her down the stairs until the last step. She stopped suddenly, and I heard Louis say excitedly, "It's there and I know it! We could be rich."

"No," said Mr. Valerie firmly.

"At least, let's…"

"I'm not interested," Mr. Valerie interrupted.

Eliza was listening as intently as I was, but when I looked at her, she turned on a fake smile and said in an extra-loud voice, "Well Addie, wasn't that fun? Seeing your old room again?" She pulled me into the living room and added to the men, "Here we are again!"

It was all done, obviously, because she didn't want me to hear the conversation between Louis and Mr. Valerie.

Louis was looking uncomfortable, like a naughty boy caught, and he was staring at me as though he wanted to see how I felt about what I'd heard.

I didn't like being left out with secrets being told behind my back and I tried not to show it.

"I asked you if you'd like a lemonade," Eliza said.

"Oh! No thank you," I answered stiffly. "I have to take a nap now. I've been sick." And with that, I walked out without saying goodbye or thanks. Louis caught up with me at the door. He put his hand on the knob and said, "Goodbye, Addie. You had a nice time, didn't you?"

"Yes," I said.

"Don't worry about anything you heard, hear? And don't tell Tom. I'll never get straight with him if he thinks I've come home for any reason other than to be with him and his mother." Louis kept his hand on the knob and waited for me to answer.

"I won't tell him anything," I said miserably, wondering what exactly I wasn't to tell.

"I know you won't tell, Addie! I know you wouldn't want Tom hurt." Louis kept his hand on the knob. "Do you promise not to tell, Addie?"

"I promise." It would be a cinch. I didn't know anything

to tell.

He took his hand off the knob and I scooted off.

After I got home I thought about what Louis might be up to and whether or not it could be bad. Was he bad? Then I thought: If Louis had never done anything wrong, if he'd stayed home, and gone downtown to the office every day, he'd have gotten fat on Aunt Mabel's good cooking and only interested in what went on in the newspaper. When he smiled, it would have been a happy ordinary smile without that mysterious little twist at the end; he'd have been exactly like Uncle Henry—old and uninteresting and definitely not my type. What he'd done, he was sorry for now, anyhow, and if he was going to do something else bad, it wasn't my business. I could feel Aunt Eveline anxiously trying to reach me, but having thought things through, I hung up on her, got out a pencil and paper, and made the table I'd read of in *Dearest* called the "Pros and Cons of True Love."

	Personality	Looks	Sincerity	Desirability	Availability	Total
Leonard	7	9	?	9	½	25 ½
Louis	10	10	?	10	?	30
Tom	7	6	10	5	10	38

Conclusions: Tom by a landslide. The only trouble was, he only won because I knew him well enough to fill in all the blanks which I couldn't for the others: The results were inaccurate. For instance, if Louis was sincere and was available, he'd beat Tom. But Leonard wouldn't beat Louis. No one would beat Louis if he was sincere and available. Therefore, he was my choice if I could just find out about those two things.

I made two more tables out of *Dearest*:

How to Test Sincerity

Method	Disadvantages	Advantages
1. Ask other people who know him well.	They might be prejudiced and insincere themselves.	I already know what people think.
2. Pay attention, wait for clues; if he says anything that can be verified, check it out.	Takes too long.	Solid proof without sticking my neck out.
3. Set a trap.	I might fall in myself.	If it worked I could find out right away.

How to Test Availability

Method	Disadvantages	Advantages
1. Ask him.	Embarrassing.	None.
2. Ask him indirectly.	Possibility of misleading if he's insincere.	None.
3. Trick him.	I'm insincere.	If I succeed he's mine.

I studied my tables and decided on a course of action, which I named T and T for Trick and Trap and changed to TNT because it sounds the same and means dynamite, which I intended my plan to be.

Seven

I woke up early Saturday morning trying to remember something I'd heard Louis say. I dragged it to the front of my mind. While we were still at lunch he'd said to Aunt Mabel he was willing to chaperone our dance with her. She hadn't said yes or no. He'd said, "My future looks bleak. How can I get anywhere before Christmas?"

"Why don't you go ahead and leave now?" she'd asked coldly.

He might have left already! I rushed to my window. There, in the early morning light, I could see the outline of Louis's car, black against the gray morning. I breathed a sigh of relief.

I heard distant thunder and smelled rain. The sky was heavy with clouds so low they almost rested on the rooftops. There was no time to lose. I thought for a minute and decided on TNT #3.

If I could make Louis like me before tonight, I might not have to worry about being a wallflower at the dance. I got out my watercolor pad and my paints and put everything else I needed in the nice little carrying-case fitted with compartments that Aunt Eveline had given me. The easel she had bought me was sturdy and heavy, and I could just manage to fit through my door and muffle the bumping by dragging it along the carpeted stairs.

The house was absolutely quiet as I tiptoed to the front door. I could hear the milkman delivering two bottles at the back. I waited until he'd come around, and I heard his truck drive off. I wanted to be sure when I passed Tom's house, there'd be no doubt about what I was planning to do and how difficult it would be to do it without a car and driver.

The easel proved to be not only a visual sign of need but an audible call for help: it made a steady thump as I dragged it along the sidewalk. It is difficult to look good lugging a six-foot, triangular-shaped wood frame, but I did my best as I passed Three Twenty and slowed down in front of Louis' car. No one seemed to be stirring in Tom's house, but I knew Aunt Mabel must be up making breakfast and that Tom would be in the back with Pumpkin, and Louis, hopefully, hovering near the front of the house. So where were they all? The first drops of rain splattered against the magnolia leaves in Tom's yard. I let the easel fall. It made a satisfying crash. I bent to pick it up, sure that someone— please, Aunt Eveline, let it be Louis—would be looking out a window to see what had happened.

"Addie! What are you doing?" Uncle Malvern opened the front door. He was dressed in a blue silk robe, his gray hair sticking out like electric wires.

"I'm going painting," I shouted, hoping my voice was carrying into the house, "but this easel wasn't meant to be carried." I looked meaningfully at Louis' car.

"Let me help you!" Uncle Malvern said, closing the door and walking toward me in the robe.

"No, no," I cried. "I'm O.K.! Thank you!" I picked up the easel and was about to move along when I saw something black flapping along the sidewalk toward me. It was Sister Maurice, hurrying in my direction. Her ground-length habit, swept by a gust of wind, flew around, making her look like a large blind bat caught in the daylight. I had the distinct feeling Aunt Eveline had sent her.

"Addie! Yoo-hoo, Addie!" she called, half a block. "You're just the person I want to see!"

Tom's door opened again. This time Louis was there. He was dressed in a smartly pressed business suit. His white shirt against his slightly tanned skin and his folded black umbrella made him look like an ad from Esquire.

"What are you doing, Addie?" he said, smiling. "Is it moving day?"

"For Chrissake, Addie!" said Tom rounding the corner of the house with Pumpkin on her leash. "You can't carry that thing. What is it, anyway?"

"It's an easel," I said. TNT #3 was turning into a convention. "I'm going painting in the park," I said, looking straight at Louis.

"I thought I could carry this but—I'm too weak."

"Weak in the head," said Tom rudely. "It's about to storm."

"You don't even need it," said Sandra Lee, appearing out of nowhere by her magical ability to be in the right place at the wrong time. "You never used an easel like that before when you painted in the park," she added suspiciously.

Uncle Malvern was staring thoughtfully at the easel. "It might work," he said.

"Yes, yes, it would." I picked up on that right away. "It's just what I need, what I've been missing every other time in the park." I gave Sandra Lee a look.

"I was thinking," said Uncle Malvern, "that it's exactly the right shape and height to hold the pipe that carries the water to the propeller of my new Time Machine!"

I looked at Louis. My heart skipped a beat; Louis was looking straight at me, and there was a twinkle in his eyes and a mysterious smile on his lips. I smiled back, and he opened his mouth to say something, but the voice that beat him to it belonged to Sister Maurice.

"Why, yes, Malvern! And hello everyone! I can just imagine how helpful a sturdy easel would be holding a pipe, and Addie certainly won't need it for what I have in mind!" She beamed at me, unchecked by the worst glance I dared turn on her. "Addie, dear, Sister Neeley and I have been planning an exciting change in this year's 'Star of Bethlehem.'" Sister Maurice paused. I continued to pump ice water into my glare.

"Do you remember that lovely Cecil B. DeMille film on the life of Christ that showed Mary with black hair instead of golden curls? Well, of course, golden curls are lovely, but Mary did have *black* hair, really, and we have decided to put Realism into our little production: real straw on the stable floor, live animals milling around." She glanced fleetingly at Pumpkin, but I could see he was rejected. "That kind of thing," Sister Maurice continued. "I don't think we can manage an actual donkey for you to ride on but, there—I've given the surprise away, haven't I?! We want you to play Our Lady this year instead of Sandra Lee! Sandra Lee, dear, of course, we have a very special role for you too! We thought that with your lovely curls, so like a halo, you would be the perfect angel for the Annunciation scene. And Addie, after that excellent theme you wrote on God is Love, we decided you could help rewrite the play with Realism and Scope. We intend to cover all the early years, not just the Birth, and it all has to be done now so that we can start rehearsal Monday morning. So you see, dear, you don't need the easel after all."

"Uh," I said.

"Shall we run along?" said Sister Maurice, "before it pours down rain? I'm sure Sandra Lee will be happy to bring your paint box home for you, and, of course, Louis and Tom can help Malvern carry his easel upstairs."

"Uh," I said. Louis and Malvern stepped up obediently.

"Take my umbrella, Sister," said Louis, almost clicking his heels.

He and Uncle Malvern picked up what had suddenly ceased to be my property, and Tom, a huge, mean grin on his face, took my paints, bent close to my ear and whispered, "Don't worry about the donkey for the play. There used to be a suit in the Great Catch-all and I know just who can fill out the back half of you!" He wiped the smile off his face, glanced at his father, and with the mean look still in his eyes whispered, "See you around, Queen of Heaven." To Sandra Lee, who was standing in shock at having been demoted from Mary to Gabriel, he said, "Come on, Sandra Lee."

"Yes, Tom!" said Sandra Lee, snapping out of her coma and batting her eyelashes at Tom. "Bye, Addie! See you at the dance tonight!"

I could hardly believe what was happening to me as Sister Maurice opened Louis' umbrella, and caught me by the arm. We blew down the sidewalk, and she talked happily about throwing away the slightly clipped, silver-painted papier-mâché star we always hung over Bethlehem, in favor of a real electric light bulb surrounded by five points in tin foil. Oh, Aunt Eveline, I thought, Help! I will be the wallflower of the evening! Not even Tom will dance with me. But there was no way out. Sister Maurice had me firmly in tow.

Everybody on the block, boys and girls together, had gone to St. Rita's grammar school through eighth grade. After that we had separated; the boys went to Jesuit and the girls to Our Lady. Jesuit was far away, and you had to take two street cars unless you wanted to ride your bike fast for twenty-five minutes, like Tom did. And Jesuit was strict; once Tom had to copy a whole column of the phone book including the dots just because he came three minutes after morning mass had started. Things were different at Our Lady. There, you could substitute French for Latin and get by with just about anything, if you did it in a ladylike fashion. Naturally, that put Sandra Lee, who couldn't add and subtract without using her fingers, at the top of the class.

Our Lady was right next to St. Rita's, part of it, really, and the same nuns taught in both places, so that you had the feeling you hadn't gone anywhere when you got to Our Lady. Sister Maurice, as Aunt Toosie put it, had been "guiding" us since first grade. At the moment, she was dragging me up the steps of the convent, which was really just a regular house a block from Aunt Toosie's.

As soon as we came in the porch door, Sister Neeley said, "Oh, thank goodness you found Addie! Addie, we are having the most difficult time with Realism and Scope! How can we possibly get girls inside sackcloth to look like real camels?"

"We could let the kings walk in and just say the camels were outside," I said.

"Why, yes! We could! That would solve the problem—but—girl kings are not Realism either."

"We could have real boys for kings," I said. Uppermost in my mind was revenge on Tom for helping wreck TNT #3. "We could borrow from Jesuits. We could have real boys in all the male parts." I let this sink in. "I know a perfect Joseph."

"Addie, you're a genius!" cried Sister Maurice. "Let's get to work on that script! Who do you want for Joseph, dear?"

I spent a happy, rainy morning creating a talkative Joseph, and I convinced Sister Maurice and Sister Neely that Tom was the only boy who could possibly memorize all those lines and play the part. Since Sandra Lee was very corporeal, a word we had just been studying in Religion, I suggested an angel would be more convincing if her voice came from offstage and she did not appear at all. It was agreed that I still had to let my hair grow as long as possible, and that Sister Maurice would personally explain the need to Aunt Toosie, since Aunt Toosie was very fussy about hair.

There used to be a costume at Three Twenty with a realistic bull's head that I told Sister Maurice about. It had belonged to Uncle Ben when he was the Beouf Gras at Mardi Gras, and I was pretty sure it was still in the Great Catch-all. Aunt Eveline had made it herself out of papier-mâché. If we cut a window in the stable scenery, we could hang the head over it, and we wouldn't need a person playing a four-legged animal.

Scope was also compromised by ending the play with

the arrival of the Wise Men and omitting the scene with Mary on a donkey being led into Egypt by Joseph. I had thought of a better role for Louis than the back of a donkey. I convinced Sister Maurice and Sister Neeley that a good play needed a good producer. Louis could be our own Cecil B. DeMille. It would give him an excuse to stay in New Orleans, and a chance to impress on Aunt Mabel and Tom that he had changed and could be a real husband and father.

All in all, the morning was a success, even if it had worked out in a different way from my plan. When I left, the sun was out, and Sister Maurice came with me as far as Tom's house to talk to Tom and Louis. I went on alone with a growing sinking feeling. The trouble was that even revenge wasn't sweet enough to make up for the fact that ahead of me loomed the Junior Debs Dance.

As I walked past Three Twenty, I was so busy trying to figure out how to get out of going I didn't notice Norma Jean until she called, "Addie!"

"Norma Jean! You're back from the hospital"

She was standing on her porch.

"Yes," she said happily. "The tests were O.K., and I can go back to Oakwood!"

"You can? When are you leaving?"

Her face fell. "Eliza thinks we ought to stay awhile so I can have the experience of a real school! What's Our Lady like?"

"It's O.K. For a school, Our Lady's not too bad." So

Eliza was not going to give up easily.

"I wish I didn't have to go," Norma Jean said.

I had never gone to a new school, but I could imagine how awful it would be to walk into a room full of strangers, especially when you were as skinny and different-looking as Norma Jean, and when a plantation had always been home to you.

"Don't worry about it," I said. "I'll go with you the first time. And you can be in the play. I'll write in a part for you," I said generously.

"What about the dance?" Norma Jean asked, without thanking me. "Will you introduce me to some boys?"

"Er—Tom's the only one I know really well," I said. How could I introduce her to Leonard when I wasn't even sure he knew me? "Junior Debs is pretty awful," I continued. "The best thing will be to pretend you're sick and maybe your father will let you stay home. I have to go because I got sick last time, and no one will believe me again!"

"Eliza will make me go no matter what I do. She's always pushing me to go out and make friends—so she can have my father all to herself."

"Well, then," I said "the next best thing to do is hide in the powder room at the dance. If the chaperones don't find you, you'll be safe. I have to go do something with my hair. Goodbye, Norma Jean!" Norma Jean didn't answer. I knew she was worrying about Eliza, and so was I. Eliza seemed to want all the men to herself.

Eight

The white sides of the Junior Debs program card stared up at me: two whole shining pages bright with twelve white empty spaces to be filled with boys' names. I'd never make it. How many dances could I hide in the powder room before the chaperones found me and dragged me out?

I could count on Tom for one dance—exactly one—if he wasn't too mad at me. He hated this as much as I did, but he could just slouch around avoiding the chaperones, since boys did all the asking. I, on the other hand, had to stand on the sidelines in full view of God and the world, in this dumb dress with too many ruffles, and my hair too long to be cute and too short to be glamorous, and everyone would know that no one wanted to dance with Adelaide Agnew. The music was starting! A horrible wave of panic washed over me, carrying me to the door in a rush. Just as I was about to make a permanent exit to freedom, I felt a firm hand on my arm.

"Addie, I've been looking for you everywhere," Louis smiled down at me. He was positively gorgeous in a real dinner coat with a snow-white shirt and a black bow-tie. Did the Salvation Army lend tuxedos?

"I—I was going to the powder room," I stammered, hiding my program in back of me and praying he wouldn't ask to see it.

He held on to me and looked into my eyes.

"I'll come back. Really," I said. Somebody must have told him that it was the chaperone's duty to push all the boys out of the corners and keep all the girls lined up where they could be seen.

"Addie, I just wanted to ask you for a dance. That is, if you have any left." I closed my mouth, which had fallen open. He wasn't being sarcastic! I grabbed at my poise. "Maybe the second dance is free?" he continued. "When you come back from the powder room?"

"Thank you, Louis," I said. "Let's see now." I held my program close to my nose and pretended to study it.

"Um. The second dance is taken, but the third dance, maybe?" That way, I could stay in the powder room for the first two dances, and there'd only be nine dances left after Louis left me. Eight, actually counting the one Tom would ask me for.

Louis made a little mocking bow and said, "The third dance, then, fair lady!"

I made myself walk slowly toward the powder room. Too slowly. The biggest drip at the dance, Livingstone Rudway III, had seen me and was hurrying across the floor in my direction. A dance with him was the one thing worse than standing alone; it was the kiss of death. I walked faster, and almost ran into Sandra Lee.

How was it possible that a dumb girl like Sandra Lee, who had never made higher than a C in any subject, could talk non-stop and say things that bowled over the captain of Jesuit's football team? Look at him—Leonard couldn't take his eyes off her! While I, who made A's in everything, couldn't think of a single sentence to say to a boy. There is definitely something wrong with the educational system in this country and—

"Addie!" cried Livingstone, panting up behind me. "May I have this dance?"

"Uh, oh," I said. Besides being the biggest drip, he didn't even know it. It never occurred to him that I'd rather fall into a snake pit than dance with him, and before I could say no, his arm was around me and we were dancing, if you call two people pushing and pulling each other dancing.

"Hey, Addie, I know a great 'Knock Knock' joke! I made it up. Do you want to hear it?"

"Uh," I said.

"Knock Knock!" said Livingstone happily.

"Who's there?" I said automatically.

"Hirohito!"

"Hirohito who?"

"Hirohito dumb to win!" yelled Livingstone. "I made it up myself! Get it, Addie? You see, Hirohito's the Emperor of Japan, and if we fight Japan, *he's too dumb* to win! Get it?"

"I've got it, Livingstone," I said wondering how anyone

so awful could be real.

"I know another one!" Livingstone was so delighted with himself he could hardly speak. "Knock Knock!"

"I'm out," I said flatly.

"Oh, Addie! You're a card, you really are! I could dance with you forever!"

"Ouch, you're on my toe!" I yelled.

"Oh, sorry. Excuse me." There was a slight pause in the conversation while we concentrated on avoiding each other's toes. "What do you think of the draft, Addie?" said Livingstone finally.

"Draft? What draft?" Leonard looked like he was going to fall down and adore Sandra Lee. "I don't feel a draft."

"Ha, ha! You're a great comedian, Addie! I mean conscription."

I looked at him blankly. "Oh. It's O.K., if it doesn't catch me."

Livingstone laughed loudly in his ghastly falsetto. "Addie, you ought to be on the radio, you really should. You're so much fun to be with!" He clasped me tighter, his clammy palm on my bare back, his pimply cheek pressing mine.

Aunt Eveline, I prayed, if ever you cared about me, prove it! Deliver me from this creep.

"Livingstone, may I break in?" I looked around and saw a white shirt. High above it was Leonard's face. I wondered if I should fall to my knees in gratitude to God and Aunt

Eveline. I was completely unprepared for a miracle on the dance floor, but for once in my whole life, I did the right thing. I didn't say no or do anything. I was even in control of my facial muscles and so relieved I was able to make my mouth smile without wobbling it. I took a deep breath as Leonard smiled back confidently and said, "You sure look cute tonight, Addie!"

Cute! Leonard had said I looked cute! Breathless and speechless, I smiled up at him. I looked cute to Leonard! It was all I could do to keep from stumbling over his feet, which seemed to be everywhere, but it didn't matter, and in a way it was good, because I had to concentrate so hard, I forgot to be shy. By the end of the dance I was so pleased I had made it without tripping that I was able to give him a big, happy smile.

"You're a great dancer, Addie," said Leonard. "I don't guess you have any more dances free, do you?"

Dearest, page 54, I was positive.

"As a matter of fact, Leonard," I said, batting my eyelashes, "I turned down somebody for the last dance because I was so hoping you'd ask me." I lowered my eyes.

Right on the mark.

"Did you really, Addie? I can hardly believe it! Can I have the last dance, then?"

"Sure!" I said. "Bye now, Leonard! Thanks awfully!"

"I hope they play 'Stardust' for the last dance, Addie," he called. "Our dance!"

In blind happiness, I bumped into Tom. "Stardust?!" he said. "Our dance? What's all that about?"

I smiled happily. He looked miserable.

"You're dancing with Leonard twice?" he asked. "Can I have this dance?"

"So sweet of you, Tom, but it's taken," I answered. I needed Tom for later.

"Well, how about the one after this?"

"Oh, I'm terribly sorry but I'm dancing with Lou—your father, that dance." I made a quick calculation: Tom would ask me for the one after that, leaving only seven dances between Tom and Leonard. But I hadn't counted on Tom's reaction.

"He asked you to dance?!" Tom yelled.

"Why not?" I said.

"Because he's an old man," said Tom, loud enough for Louis, who was coming towards us, to hear. Louis looked surprised and hurt, then he smiled and said, "Hello, young man, I believe this is my dance with Addie?"

"Yeah," said Tom, turning away. "You can have her; you and my good friend, Leonard."

There went my dance with Tom, and Louis was one dance early. I would have to disappear for nine whole dances.

As Louis swept me out on the dance floor, I tried desperately to think of something to say. Look at Sandra Lee, still talking! Was she repeating herself? Why—she was dancing with Tom! And there he was hanging on her every word! He never danced with anyone but me!

Suddenly, I realized Louis had asked me something.

"Er—ah—what did you say?"

"I was saying that I've been remembering a few things, and that years ago, I left something I cared about at Three Twenty. It wasn't important, but I liked it, and I wondered if you'd ever come across it when you moved?"

"What is it?"

"It was a small wooden box I had as a child, nothing really important, something from the East—China, I think. It smelled nice like cedar, and had a little painting of a snow-capped mountain on the top—Fujiyama, I guess. It must have been Japanese. I hardly remember, but when I was older, I gave it to your Aunt Eveline—for her birthday or some such occasion."

"Oh, I do remember it! Aunt Eveline used to keep it on her dresser."

"And you played with it!?"

"Oh, no, Aunt Eveline would never have given it to me to play with."

"Where is it, do you know? Do you have it?" he asked.

"No, I don't. I don't remember what happened to it. Maybe Aunt Toosie let it go to the Salvation Army, or she might have put it in the Great Catch-all."

"The Great Catch-all? You mean the armoire Simeon was talking about?"

"Yes, the armoire in the attic that we're going to go through. I remember the box wasn't on Aunt Eveline's dresser when she died, so maybe it needed mending and she put it there."

"You mean to say that Toosie really never sorted out all of your Aunt Eveline's things?"

"Oh, she went through all of the important stuff. It's just that the Great Catch-all was full of junk, nothing important, and she was so busy and tired and she always meant to go through it; she just didn't. And then the people that moved in were older. It would have been kind of awkward because we didn't know them well. It wasn't important—except—I can't wait to see what is still in the Great Catch-ALL!"

"Well now, it might be a mistake! No good digging up the past, Addie. Look to the future!" Louis had stopped dancing and was staring at me. "People say you learn from the past," he continued, "but I say if you keep looking back, you stumble in the future."

"Aunt Eveline used to say you build on the past and grow into the future. That's not the same as looking back." I was puzzled. Didn't he want to go through the Great Catch-all with me?

"You might know she would have said something like that," Louis mumbled, remembering to dance again.

"Didn't you like my Aunt Eveline?" I had heard sarcasm in his voice.

"I admired her very much," Louis said.

Which is not the same thing, I thought.

"Addie, I'll tell you what. We'll make a definite date to dig into the past together. Some time next week. And we'll look for some of the costumes you need for the play. Maybe we'll find my box. How does that suit you?"

It suited me just fine. Anything I did with Louis suited me.

"Monday," I said. "I'll ask the Valeries if we can go in their attic after school. I'll tell them I want to look for costumes for the play."

"O.K., but we don't have to be in such a hurry all of a sudden. I'm staying here a while. Sister Maurice asked me to be the director of the play, and I thought it might be an opportunity to be with Tom. How do you see it, Addie?" he asked. "Is there any hope?"

"Oh, yes," I said, "but some day you'll have to tell him about where you've been all this time." I waited to see if he'd tell me, but he didn't say a word. "It won't work with Tom, trying to *talk* him into loving you," I continued. "You've got to show him, and be honest with him."

"How?" asked Louis.

"All you have to do is be around," I said, "and if you're the director, you'll be around. Then, maybe after you've made him like you, you can tell him about—everything."

We were standing in the middle of the dance floor almost alone. Louis didn't seem to notice. "You've convinced me, Addie," he said. "I'll make use of the role of Cecil B. DeMille in the production of 'Star of Bethlehem'. And now may I lead you to your partner."

"Er, no, thank you," I said nervously. Louis' problems were solved; mine had arrived. "Thanks," I said, my eye on the powder room. While people tried to find their partners, I sprinted to the door and pushed. It was stuck! I shoved. No, it wasn't stuck, it was jam-packed and overflowing with refugees from the dance floor. There wasn't one girl in there that wasn't either fat, homely, or dressed like the 1890's. I threaded my way quickly and wordlessly through the fake gaiety into one of the toilets and locked the door. I closed the seat, climbed on and sat down with my long dress and my feet tucked under me. With luck, no one would know where I'd been until the last dance.

My plan contained one major flaw. How was I to know when dance twelve started? I couldn't even hear the music except when the door opened. I'd have to listen to conversations for clues.

It was an eternity, and I had time to solve the problems of the whole world, but I was too busy listening for clues in the endless chapter about everything except what dance was going on. I was just about to come out, figuring it was close to #12. As I unwound, I found my ankles ached from sitting on them and one foot was asleep. Suddenly, I heard a familiar voice:

"Whew! I'm exhausted," cried Sandra Lee, bursting

through the door.

"My feet are killing me," shrieked her companion happily. "I've danced every dance." It had to be Becky, the only other really popular girl.

"My program was full before I even got here," said Sandra Lee. "It always is."

"Where's your cousin Addie?" asked Becky in a catty tone.

"Oh, poor Addie! She only danced once with one of the chaperones," said my loyal cousin. "Unless you count the dance she had with that creep, Livingstone. I think she left right after that."

"I saw Addie dancing with Leonard," said Becky, even cattier.

"Oh, that doesn't count—it was because I felt sorry for Addie and sent him over to her," said Sandra Lee. "He'd do anything for me."

"He would not!" I yelled, forgetting I'd locked myself in, and banging my nose against the door trying to get out. "Leonard asked me for the last dance, the best dance of all, so there!"

"Well, then," said Sandra Lee coolly, "he must have changed his mind. I just danced the last dance with him. Stardust."

"The dance is over?" I wailed. "Stardust?!"

"You've been hiding in here the whole time!" Sandra Lee said, delighted.

I tried to think of something to say, but *Dearest* didn't cover this situation.

While I stood there, Sandra Lee and Becky powdered their noses, which weren't shiny, combed their hair, which shone and bounced perfectly before they'd even started, and chatted happily together, ignoring me.

"So long, Addie," said Sandra Lee on the way out. "I'm spending the night at Becky's." The door slammed shut.

"Ow," I groaned. Behind me, I heard a noise. I spun around, and there stood Norma Jean in one of those long dresses with a starched petticoat, which is supposed to make you look like a Southern Belle but actually makes you look like a pin cushion.

"I was hiding too, Addie," said Norma Jean. "For all twelve dances. My father's going to bring me home. Do you want a ride?"

"Yes," I said humbly.

It turned out we rode home in Louis' car, me in the front seat with Louis, and Norma Jean and her father in back. I'd plotted and planned, trying to get myself into exactly this position. Here I was sitting with Louis in the front seat of his car. I had all of his attention. He was talking comfortably to me, and I was answering in monosyllables like an idiot. So, what was wrong? I wasn't Dolores, that was the problem. I was just plain Addie, and Louis had only danced with me because—how should I know? Leonard had danced with me because he felt sorry for me and Tom—I was a traitor.

Tom would never forgive me.

"Ow!" I wailed involuntarily.

"What did you say, Addie?" Louis asked.

"Nothing," I mumbled.

"Simeon just asked if you'd like to spend the night at Three Twenty," Louis said. "You girls could have a slumber party and giggle all night."

"Louis and I could get your old bed down from the attic," Mr. Valerie added.

"My very own bed!" I forgot my unhappy love life. "I'd love to come!"

"That would be nice, Addie!" Even Norma Jean managed a little enthusiasm.

"I'll ask the minute I get home, but Aunt Toosie lets me do anything!"

"Louis, the evening's young," said Mr. Valerie. "Why don't you and Mabel join us for a nightcap after you and I move the bed?"

"I'll ask her," said Louis, "but I doubt she'll come. I'll try."

"Yes, try," said Mr. Valerie. "Do her good."

I burst into Aunt Toosie's room the minute I got back.

"My, you look so happy. You must have had a lovely time!" she said. "I'll bet you danced every dance!"

"Yes, lovely!" I lied without even thinking. "Aunt Toosie, may I spend the night at Three Twenty? They're going to get *my* bed down from the attic and put it in *my* room and oh—please can I go?"

Of course, she said yes, and even though it was eleven o'clock at night, I went hurrying over to Tom's to be sure Louis was coming to help move the bed. As I got near, I could hear the porch swing squeaking and voices talking low. I had come too close to leave without being seen.

"Ahem," I said loudly. The voices went on talking, and there was nothing to do but step out of sight behind the oleander bush.

"Louis, I'm not coming. You hoped I'd say no," Aunt Mabel whined.

"That's not so! Can't you believe I came back to New Orleans because I wanted to try again?"

"After ten years?! No, I think you came back for something to do with money."

"There! I told you, Mabel. It's not just the past you can't forgive, it's the future as well. I might have known how bitter you'd be."

"Bitter?! I have every right to be bitter!"

"Yes, of course you do," said Louis wearily, "and I hope you enjoy it, because God knows the only other thing you seem to enjoy is being right. Suppose I did come back because of money?"

Aunt Mabel laughed in an ugly way. "No one has money around here."

"I see an opportunity to make money here," said Louis. "I could make a fortune. But Mabel, the real reason I came back was because of you and Tom. Wait now, Mabel!" he said as Aunt Mabel started to interrupt. "Listen. A year ago I had fallen about as low as a man can. I won't bore you with the details. Mostly, it was just plain bad luck. You wouldn't even have recognized me; ragged, dirty clothes, a stubble on my chin. I was literally picked up on Sunday morning by the Salvation Army, brought to their settlement house in New York, washed, fed, and clothed. Clothed—that was it! The incredible coincidence! I was clothed in Eveline's brother's suit—still had his name tag, 'Ben Woods', in it, although I think I might have recognized it as Ben's even without the label! How it got all the way to New York is a miracle—but there I was, dressed in an expensive light gray wool with pinstripes, cut by Henry, the tailor. Ten years old and a little worn, but still very elegant. Only the best for Ben!"

"So what was amazing about that? It was just a coincidence," Aunt Mabel said.

"It was in a whole box of things that had come from Three Twenty, including some of Eveline's dresses. Don't you think that's miraculous? All the way to New York? But the most important part was an old newspaper clipping— her death notice—she'd been gone almost a year by the time I read it, and I hadn't even known Ben was dead. I was standing there in the basement, sorting clothes and everything that people had sent from all over the country, and here was my bit of New Orleans, my old life back to haunt and tempt me. I'll never believe it was pure coincidence."

"Are you trying to say that God sent you back to me, then? Is that it?" Aunt Mabel said sarcastically.

"All right." Louis sighed heavily and got up. "I give up."

But Aunt Mabel was too wound up to stop. "You never did anything in your whole life that didn't have money for a motive!" she shouted. "You married me for money, only my father lost it all in the crash before you could get your hands on it!"

If Aunt Mabel wanted Louis, why did she say those horrible things to him?

"My, my, the years have made you cynical, Mabel!" Louis said. "Well, I'll not give in so easily. Tom needs me, whether he knows it or not."

"Tom's done just fine without you!" Aunt Mabel screamed. "You—you—I know what you're up to!"

"Oh, the truth finally comes out," Louis said.

I wasn't sure I was ready for the truth. This was already more than I wanted to hear. I slipped out of the oleander bush. But I couldn't get away quickly enough, and I heard Aunt Mabel yell, "You're having an affair, that's what!"

"With whom, pray tell," said Louis angrily.

"With Eliza!" Aunt Mabel shouted hysterically, as I walked rapidly backwards.

I was safely out of their sight when Louis started to laugh wildly, and I ran away before I could hear his answer.

Nine

Adultery. That was what an affair was. The word wasn't even mentioned in *Dearest*. The only place I'd seen it written was in the Ten Commandments, and Sister Maurice always managed to skirt around it in "the examination of conscience" we went through before going to Confession. "Have you had any impure thoughts?" we were supposed to ask ourselves, and you could tell by the looks on everybody's face that the sixth commandment was number one on their conscience.

I sneaked back through Tom's yard, hoping Pumpkin wouldn't start barking. I wasn't sure I could love a man who'd committed adultery. The moon was full, and clouds raced across it. I heard Pumpkin's tail thumping on the shed floor; he'd seen and recognized me.

Would Mr. Valerie divorce Eliza if it were true? I didn't really think so. I'd seen him look at Eliza, and Norma Jean would just have to get used to the fact that her father was madly in love with his wife. But where did that leave me? Why were everybody's problems easier to figure out than mine?

Pumpkin whined for attention. "Shut up, Pumpkin," I

said, "I'm thinking." It was hopeless; I couldn't compete with anyone as sophisticated and gorgeous as Eliza. I couldn't even get anywhere with boys my age. Supposed Tom said something to Leonard about the dance, something like, "What do you mean by dancing with my girlfriend?"

Leonard might answer, "I just danced with her because I felt sorry for her." My cheeks burned with shame at the thought.

Out of the corner of my eye, I saw someone dart through the hedge between Tom's and Three Twenty. I figured it must be Louis going over to help Mr. Valerie with my bed, so I followed him through the hedge to the kitchen door of Three Twenty. It was open, and I went in. I didn't see anyone, but I heard Mr. Valerie and Eliza talking to Louis in the dining room. I ran up the familiar back steps to the upstairs hall. Norma Jean's door was closed, and I found myself next to the attic door. I opened it a crack and looked up the steps. The feeling that something there was waiting for me was strong. I remembered it so clearly I could hear Aunt Eveline saying again, "Adelaide, I don't want you in the attic. There are loose floor boards and all kinds of things that could hurt you." I put my foot deliberately on the first step and closed the door carefully behind me.

I tiptoed up the steps to the top. The attic was huge, with dark recesses packed full of strange-shaped boxes. I remembered the old broken grandfather clock with its ominous bong that had echoed as you walked by it. Now, standing in its place was a strange wire figure with an hourglass shape. Draped with fabric, it was the same size as Eliza, and I had the feeling it was an extra sense of hers spying on me. I hurried past the wire model and saw my homey brass bed and mattress in a corner waiting for me. I sat on it and bounced once. It had a familiar, welcoming feel, an invitation to snuggle into the past. I could hardly wait.

Facing me was the Great Catch-all, as forbidding as my bed was welcoming. It was the size of a small shed, made of mahogany and varnished so many times it was dark black and lusterless. There were two doors: one side had shelves, and the other hanging space. I walked over to it and put my hand out to turn the key on the shelf side. I stopped, arm outstretched. The door on the hanging side had creaked. Slowly, slowly, it began to swing open as though some weak thing inside wanted to come out. Run, Addie, run, I thought, but I was stuck, glued to the floor.

I heard a stifled squeal and realized it was coming from me. The door was open, the hanging costumes swaying, ready to float out in a phantom Mardi Gras ball! The costumes parted, and in the middle of my scream, Uncle Malvern's face appeared between a clown suit and black cape!

In my mind I knew it was only safe, old Uncle Malvern, but my mind wasn't in control, and I was shrieking.

"Sh-sh, Addie!" he stage-whispered, fingers to his lips.

His face looked ridiculous in a wide-eyed expression.

Mr. Valerie came crashing up the stairs, but not before Uncle Malvern had invented a story.

"Addie saw a mouse" he said. "Sorry we disturbed you. We were just going through the armoire—for Toosie, you know. At last." He didn't explain why he had chosen the middle of the night or neglected to ask Mr. Valerie's permission to enter the house. Mr. Valerie probably thought that somehow he'd come with me to move the bed. Continuing non-stop, Uncle Malvern said, "Such a fright! You know how girls are about mice! Ha, ha!"

I was so weak and relieved, I didn't mind appearing to be a silly girl, afraid of a little mouse.

"Did you see all the costumes?" Mr. Valerie asked me.

"I forgot to look," I said stupidly, and turned to open the shelf side of the armoire. It wasn't scary any more, and there was the Boeuf Gras head exactly where I'd thought it would be, but I certainly wasn't interested in it now.

"You can look for costumes at a more appropriate time," Mr. Valerie said dryly. "Louis and I are going to carry Addie's bed downstairs, Malvern."

"Thank you, thank you," Uncle Malvern babbled. "I'll come back when Addie is feeling more up to snuff. That's very kind of you."

I tried to smile politely, and I let Uncle Malvern help me down the stairs his hand on my elbow. I had ceased to care about costumes, the Great Catch-all, or even my bed.

"Uncle Malvern," I whispered, "what were you doing there?"

"Addie," he answered, "if what I think is correct, I've found an important link in the Time Machine!"

"What is it?"

"Trust me," continued Uncle Malvern. "You're too young to handle this." He patted my shoulder with his free hand and nodded wisely, hurrying the rest of the way down the steps.

Uncle Malvern broke into a trot and almost ran into Louis in the hall before darting away.

"What was that all about!?" Louis asked.

"Oh, nothing," I said. "Uncle Malvern was looking for something."

"Do you know what it was?" Louis asked, frowning.

"No," I said. "Something to do with his invention."

"You mean Malvern was already in my attic when you got there?" Eliza had walked up and was looking at me intently.

"He asked me if he could go up," said Norma Jean, standing in her doorway, cool as a cucumber. "He's looking for a very important part to his Time Machine, and he thought it might be in the Great Catch-all." If Norma Jean was lying, she carried it off with wide-eyed innocence.

"Well, well," said Louis sarcastically, "the Jules Verne of Audubon Street!"

"He is a bit off, isn't he?" said Mr. Valerie, coming down

the steps with the bottom of my bed.

"Odd?! He's nuttier than a fruit cake," said Louis. "Did he find the missing link, Addie? Are we all to be transported back into the past?"

Mr. Valerie broke in before I had to answer. "It certainly doesn't matter, in any case. The poor man will never invent anything worthwhile. Let's go back up for the mattress, Louis."

"I talked to Uncle Malvern in the garden the other day," said Norma Jean. "He's smarter than you think. I like him."

No one said anything.

"And in a way, he did transport me into the past!" she continued. "He told me a story about how he and your Uncle Ben, Addie, had visited a plantation when they were young. It sounded like Oakwood, and the way he told it made me feel like I was there with them."

"What else did he say about Ben?" Louis asked.

"That was all," said Norma Jean.

"Well, you always have had a more vivid imagination than most of us," Eliza said, making it sound like a fault. "You're always imagining things. You should play with children your own age more and not hang around by yourself so much. You should…" Uncle Malvern's mysterious visit to the attic was forgotten as Eliza, the wicked stepmother, lectured Norma Jean. Norma Jean practically crawled into the wall; I could feel her retreating more and more, until Mr. Valerie broke in.

"Good heavens, Eliza! That's enough. This isn't a schoolroom! Come on, Louis, let's get that bed downstairs."

It didn't take long to set up my bed, and Eliza made it with sheets that smelled deliciously like cedar. When she was finished, I sighed and tried to snuggle down. But the mattress felt hard, and my mind was still racing from the scare Uncle Malvern had given me and what Aunt Mabel had said to Louis.

Norma Jean didn't answer when Eliza turned out the light and said, "Good night, girls."

"Good night," I answered for both of us. I forgot about Norma Jean and closed my eyes, trying to pretend it was long ago and I was waiting for Aunt Eveline to tuck me in. But I was too grown-up for that sort of thing. That was it—I was caught in the middle, halfway between too old for being tucked in and too young to compete with a gorgeous woman. How much longer would I have to wait to grow up?

"You don't 'wait' to grow up," said Aunt Eveline. "The verb 'to grow up' implies action on your part. You do something about it."

"But I am doing something about it—as fast as I can with a slow figure. I'm trying hard to act grown-up!"

"You said it."

"Said what?"

"'Act.' Don't *act* grown-up. Be yourself. Maybe you could start by thinking about what being grown-up means.

Work on that. Good night, Addie."

But I was too tired for Aunt Eveline's kind of soul-searching. I couldn't even conjure up her ghost again, and I actually began to wish I was next door at Aunt Toosie's. The new, Early American furniture, covered with flowered chintz, was homey and comfortable. So was Aunt Toosie.

I looked at Norma Jean's organdy curtains ruffling up the moonlight on the windowsill and remembered how badly I'd wanted curtains like that when I was living in this house, but I didn't even care anymore.

"Norma Jean?" I asked, to see if she was awake. "Did Uncle Malvern really ask you if he could go in the attic?"

"Why did she have to marry my father?!" Norma Jean burst out, ignoring my question. "She hates me and Oakwood!"

"Listen, Norma Jean," I said. "It's not all that bad. Try not to worry about it." Tomorrow, I'd forget my own problems and really concentrate on Norma Jean. "Tomorrow, I'll introduce you to some of my friends," I added recklessly. I didn't know who those friends were, but I'd figure out something. Maybe I'd go up to Becky and say, "Hi, Becky, this is my friend Norma Jean!"

"Norma Jean?" I whispered. She didn't answer, but I knew she wasn't sleeping. I couldn't sleep either; I was sick of wondering if Uncle Malvern's visit to the attic made sense and who Louis really liked.

"Addie, go to sleep!" I heard Aunt Eveline say.

"Tomorrow you can get on with your painting. Good night, Addie!" Her voice seemed to be coming from my room at Aunt Toosie's.

Ten

"You missed the game and Tom caught a touchdown pass!" Sandra Lee shouted over "Begin the Beguine" blaring out of her record player. She couldn't even wait until I was within normal hearing distance. "And after the game, Tom took Becky and I to a party at Harold's!" Her curls were damp from dancing all by herself.

How could I have been so stupid? Like a dumbbell, I'd gone painting on the levee after school, and forgotten all about the game.

"Me," I said, slamming the door and banging my paints on the floor.

"Me? What are you talking about?"

"Your grammar. Leonard and Tom took Becky and me, not I."

"So what? We had a great time at Harold's. Boy, can Tom boogie-woogie!" She did a few dance steps to show me what she meant.

"That's news to me. He hates dancing," I said.

"That's what you think! He's really in the groove!"

"Are we discussing the same person?" I asked, not nearly as cool as I tried to sound. Sandra Lee finished with a twirl.

"Anyhow, we talked about going to see 'Suspicion.' It's playing at the Saenger. Cary Grant and Joan Fontaine. And Tom brought me home."

"That's logical. You live two houses away from him."

"There was more to it than that," she added coyly.

"What more?" I couldn't help asking.

"Well, I hate to tell you because I know you consider Tom your property, but..." she paused and fingered her full, peasant skirt. "The truth is—well, if I hadn't made it absolutely clear that I wasn't interested in stealing my own cousin's boyfriend, Tom would—well he would have—gone too far!"

"Gone too far! How far is that? What did you *do*?"

"Me? I mean—I—I did nothing. I was speaking of what Tom did."

"What did *he* do?" I asked in a very small voice.

"I wouldn't dream of telling! Do you think I'd tell something like that? He'd die of embarrassment."

I could feel my eyes beginning to fill. There was no way to beat Sandra Lee at her own game, but the last thing I wanted to do was let her see me cry. Suddenly, and just in time through the blur of a tear ready to fall, I saw a change. I blinked and watched Sandra Lee's face collapsing into less animated lines.

"Where were you?" she asked in very curious tones.

"That's my secret," I answered watching her carefully. Where did she think I'd been?

"Were you—I mean—well—I was just kidding about Tom. He didn't do anything much. Who were you with?"

"I can't tell," I said looking down in what I hoped was an embarrassed way.

"In fact," said Sandra Lee "I didn't have all that great a time at Harold's. I'm sick of Leonard, and Tom said he wished you'd been at the game. That was going too far!" She half laughed as I tried not to look as flabbergasted as I felt. Then she got to the point. "Were you with Louis?" Sandra Lee asked wistfully.

"Hmmm," I said, trying to look as though I had been.

"Listen Addie, how is it you're doing so well with Louis? I've tried everything in *Dearest*, and he won't look at me!"

I was stunned. Sandra Lee was after Louis, and thought I had him! The great Sandra Lee was asking my advice about men. I tried to keep up my act, but I couldn't help laughing. "Sandra Lee," I said, "if we could just have something to eat, I'll tell you all about it."

"We can make Tomato Surprise," said Sandra Lee excitedly. "Did he—he didn't—did he go too far or anything?"

"Not *yet*," I said, and added as an afterthought, "I think he respects me too much." I sliced tomatoes slowly to put under the cheese and bacon and told Sandra Lee that Aunt Mabel suspected Louis and Eliza were committing "you-know-what." I popped the sandwiches under the broiler and ignored Aunt Eveline, who was trying to get through with a message about gossiping.

"You don't mean," said Sandra Lee, her eyes wide and shining, "you don't mean you think they commit—," she gulped but couldn't say it, "you-know-what all the time?"

"Aunt Mabel thinks it's why he came home," I said knowingly.

"But where does that leave you?" Sandra Lee asked.

"I know," I said, my mouth full of melting cheese, "that's the trouble. Eliza has the advantage of experience."

Sandra Lee looked at me with new respect. "Do you think he'll be at rehearsal tomorrow?" she asked.

"Maybe." I tried to look as though I knew all about his plans. "He doesn't tell me *everything*, of course." I got up and walked across the kitchen, trying to imitate Eliza's slow, hip-swaying amble, which is difficult when you're short on hips.

It must have looked impressive, because Sandra Lee was struck dumb again. Then she said, "Eliza's tough competition! Gee, I can't wait for rehearsal tomorrow! Let's go together. I'll meet you after religion class, O.K.?"

"It's O.K. with me," I said, shrugging my shoulders indifferently. "Louis didn't ask me to go with him this time." I made it sound like he had every other time. Sandra Lee looked very impressed.

"I just can't wait for rehearsal!" she said again.

Unfortunately, the Star of Bethlehem wasn't coming

along too well. The boys from Jesuit missed rehearsals because of football practice and debate team meetings, and the girls didn't seem interested in memorizing their lines. Sandra Lee and I weren't the only ones who'd fallen for Louis. Everyone thought he was divine. He didn't even know their names, but they'd just look at him, giggle, and make Sister Maurice mad.

That afternoon Louis didn't come. When Louis wasn't there, they acted bored.

"Do you think he's committing—it?" Sandra Lee whispered to me.

"Not in the daytime," I said trying to look wise.

"Addie," Sister Maurice said, "please pay attention!" After a listless rehearsal, she called me aside. "Addie, we have to revise. The lines are too long to be either memorized or realistic. Come with me."

I gave Sandra Lee my books to take home and walked over to the convent. Sister Maurice did not give me her usual friendly smile as I sat down at the dining room table, so shiny I could see my reflection. I sat there staring at myself and glancing occasionally at Sister Maurice's earnest face as she went through the script like a scythe in the cane field, leaving bare stalks of sentences and adding lots of gestures and easy-to-memorize expressions like "Lo!" and "Hark!"

"Addie, I think the Angel of the Annunciation should be on stage after all, don't you?" Sister Maurice looked at me sternly.

"Yes, Sister Maurice," I said meekly.

I could tell she suspected me of having left Sandra Lee's golden curls out of sight on purpose.

"Have you any other suggestions for improvement?" Sister Maurice asked, watching me carefully.

"Norma Jean is supposed to have a good voice. She could sing a solo maybe."

"There's no way to go but up in the music department," said Sister Maurice. "I'll give her a chance." All the changes took forever, and by the time Sister Maurice was finished, the Star of Bethlehem had lost all of its Scope and the only thing left of Realism was my black hair.

"Addie, have you been paying attention?" Sister Maurice asked, catching me thinking about Louis.

"Oh yes, Sister Maurice. 'Glory to God in the Highest!' you said."

"There is nothing you'd like to talk to me about, is there?"

"Oh, no, Sister!" I said quickly. "Everything is just fine."

"All right then, Addie, I think the Star of Bethlehem is much better now, don't you?"

"Yes, Sister Maurice."

"You mentioned there was a mask of a cow's head—a Boeuf Gras in Norma Jean's attic. I wonder if you could get it now that we've settled for less realism."

"I'll get it on the way home, Sister Maurice," I said.

"Well, then, that's it, Addie." Sister Maurice stood up.

"I think we have something manageable now, and I'm glad we've put Sandra Lee back on stage and that you mentioned Norma Jean's voice. Goodbye and God bless you. Don't forget to pick up the Boeuf Gras at Norma Jean's."

"I'll get it first thing, Sister Maurice," I said. But when I arrived at Three Twenty, Norma Jean was on the way to the doctor with her father.

"We'll be back soon," said Mr. Valerie, helping a silent Norma Jean into his car. "Make yourself at home, Addie. You can take any of the costumes you find in the Great Catch-all. The front door's open."

I forgot to ask where Eliza was and tiptoed up the stairs, wondering if she was behind her closed door taking a nap.

"Mrs. Valerie?" It was almost a whisper and got no answer. She was probably out shopping for a gorgeous dress or something.

"I'm out too," said Aunt Eveline, angrily. "If you need me, you won't find me here. Adelaide, wait until Norma Jean gets back."

I ignored Aunt Eveline and climbed the steps to the attic.

The light was dim, and I had that old creepy feeling that things were lurking in the shadows. The only window was a small, diamond-shaped one with two stained-glass panes, and I opened it to let in more light. As I was about to turn away, I saw Louis hurrying up the walk. I froze. The front screen door slammed shut as he came in the house.

Voices. Eliza and Louis: she was calling to him from the top of the stairs, and he was coming up. She must have been in her bedroom all along, and before I could do more than scramble under my old bed, they had opened the attic door! They were heading straight for me! "Oh, please, please Aunt Eveline," I prayed, "Don't let them find me!"

"We shouldn't meet like this," Eliza said.

"I had to see you alone," said Louis passionately. If only Louis had said that to me! "Eliza, you're not doing your part!" How I yearned for Eliza's part. I would certainly do it. "Yes, I am. I can't do more without Simeon getting suspicious. Not to mention Norma Jean. She hates me, and Nini's been watching me, running over from your house, pretending to need a cup of sugar. They'd all love to have something against me. If Norma Jean found out!—that would be the end of everything!"

It is already the end of everything, I thought.

"You have to go further," Louis said. I could just imagine Louis reaching out and Eliza melting into his arms. "Let's talk this out. Sit here a moment."

"No. Let's get this over with. I thought we'd come up here to look for the box."

That's right, Louis. The *box*. You're supposed to be interested in a *box*. I tried to concentrate my powers, but I didn't have any.

"What we have to do first is more important," Louis said.

Oh, no! He was leading her toward my bed! I could see his black shoes and her small, high-heeled ones. Dear God, didn't you get the word from Aunt Eveline?! *Don't* let them find me. And please God, don't let them go all the way with me here under the bed!

"Sit here," said Louis, dragging an old chair close to the bed and plumping himself down so hard on the mattress the springs almost touched my nose. Oh, God listen to me! Aunt Eveline! Did you hear me?!

"Let's get down to business," Louis said.

Aunt Eveline! Aunt Eveline, *please!* What had happened to the Communion of Saints? The line was dead.

"Why won't you do it?" Louis asked.

Don't give in now, Eliza! Give her strength, Lord!

"I'm almost positive Nini suspects something about your past," said Eliza.

"It doesn't matter what anyone *suspects*, as long as Addie doesn't *know*."

Addie?! Me? "Mabel suspects too, for that matter," Louis continued, "but it's just their suspicious natures. It doesn't matter what she thinks."

"It does matter, Louis. This just isn't working."

"It will work," cried Louis passionately. He was going to grab Eliza. I was sure of it. "It was something only Ben knew, and when Eveline found out, she'd never have told. Not Eveline!"

I tried to imagine how Uncle Ben and Aunt Eveline fit

in at this moment.

"If we just knew for sure... I mean suppose, just suppose that girl... she could ruin everything, including me!"

"She doesn't have the box."

"Let's look and make sure it's not in that old armoire."

"Will you stop worrying? We'll look thoroughly. I've already been through it once—hastily, because Simeon was in the house and I didn't have enough time. Anyhow, I'm sure it must have been given to the Salvation Army with the rest of the stuff, but we'll look again."

He must mean the Japanese box that used to be on Aunt Eveline's dresser, but why would that have anything to do with a love affair?

"You don't suppose Malvern was looking for it?" Eliza asked.

"Of course not. He doesn't know about any of it. Besides, he's a drunk."

"I'd feel a lot better if I knew how much that girl knows! She could ruin everything if she knew—even part of the truth!"

"I realize that, Eliza! But I *promise* you: she's not going to ruin our plans."

"What *does* that mean?"

Yes, what does that mean?

"It means I'll go to any *lengths*! No little girl is going to stand in my way!" My heart sank. He thought I was a "little girl." I wondered if I was the first woman whose love life had ended under a bed.

Louis' voice grew soft, "Now, about your part," he said and sat back down on the mattress.

It was all I could do to keep from scrambling out of my hiding place to tell them it was no time for romance.

"Hurry, Eliza," he said.

"You've got to get out of here before anyone sees you," Eliza said.

"All right. We'll search the Catch-All later, but let's get down to the important business now," Louis said.

Oh God, if you are really there, Do Something!

"I want to go over this with you, carefully. The way I see it," Louis continued, "we proceed as we planned. The expert will show the sample to Simeon, and convince him of how much money it means. Your job is to manipulate the plantation books so that he'll see that without extra income, he'll never be able to hold on to Oakwood. I've drawn up this little schedule to help you with that. This is what you have to get straight. Then, after Simeon's digested it, I present him again with the idea and convince him I know what I'm talking about. It can't fail, Eliza! It's a sure thing, and we'll all be rich! Just do your part, Eliza. Here, use this table and make the plantation books look worse so that Simeon will feel the pinch and know he has to take measures."

"That's not honest."

"That's only a little cheating for the better good! Don't

you see that?"

"I guess so," Eliza said weakly. "I know that if I don't do something, he'll never agree to a gamble."

"Eliza, it's not a gamble, I tell you! It's a sure thing! There's oil on that land, I guarantee you. Don't forget I'm a geologist and I know what I'm talking about! Promise you'll take care of the books."

"I promise," said Eliza.

Louis stood up again. "O.K. I'll look for the box alone. You go down first. If the coast is clear, I'll follow you in a minute."

Lord, I thank you, I prayed weakly. Even though my love life has taken a turn for the worse, at least they didn't go all the way. They didn't even kiss! It was not adultery after all (and it was still a triangle, not a rectangle). Eliza went down the steps, and I watched Louis' shoes march to the window. The silence was deafening. How could he help hearing my heart thumping away, my breath coming in gasps? Should I scramble out and throw myself into his arms, and prove I was not a little girl? No, I decided, this was no time for love between us; it was more like the perfect time for him to take care of someone who knew too much. Louis turned from the window, and, without stopping at the armoire to hunt for the box, walked toward the steps.

I waited for a long time to move after I heard the door downstairs close. It took that long to catch my breath and figure out what I should do next. Louis had a scheme to get rich just as Aunt Mabel had thought, but what did I have to do with any of it? He had said, "As long as Addie doesn't know." Know what?

I crawled out from under the bed and dusted myself off. The box was the key to everything; I saw that. But what was in it? And if Aunt Eveline had known it was important, why hadn't she told me about it? It didn't make sense. I tried to remember what had happened to the things on Aunt Eveline's dresser. I could see the box plainly. I opened the armoire door to look for it.

I was rooting through a big box on the second shelf when suddenly, out of the corner of my eye, I caught movement and spun around.

Louis was standing between me and the attic steps.

Eleven

"Louis!" I shrieked, my own voice scaring me all the more.

"Next time you hide under a bed, remember you have feet," he said coldly. "I saw your foot sticking out after Eliza left."

"I didn't mean to hear anything," I stammered. "I was there when you came, so I had to hide. I didn't really hear anything I understood, anyhow!"

"There's the matter of the letter you have there," he said ignoring my excuses.

"What letter?" I asked innocently, looking down at the letter in my hand.

"That one," he said. "I believe it is addressed to someone other than yourself. Your Uncle Ben, if I am not mistaken."

I looked at the envelope. It was addressed to my mother in my father's handwriting. "This isn't the letter to Uncle Ben," I said.

"Where is it, then? Have you read it?"

"I haven't even opened it."

"That doesn't sound like you," said Louis suspiciously, looking me hard in the eye.

"Oh, I wouldn't read someone else's mail," I said piously,

wondering what we were talking about. "Aunt Eveline taught me never to open anyone else's mail."

"Let me have it, please." He held out his hand.

"Oh, none of these are *that* letter," I said. "These are my mother's. But the one you want belongs to Aunt Eveline. Everything of Uncle Ben's went to Aunt Eveline."

"She's dead," Louis said coldly. "I wrote the letter. It's mine. It should be destroyed."

"But it's proof—er—ah—" I guessed right.

"You have read it! Well, I knew you had. But it all happened a long time ago and the whole thing was taken care of. I want to tear up the letter—to protect Tom and Mabel."

He was lying. He didn't want anyone to read the letter because there was something in it that could still hurt him.

"Where is it?"

"It's back at Aunt Toosie's." I made a wild guess. "In the little Japanese box."

"So you had the box all along. How did you open it without a key?"

It was amazing how much I was finding out by pretending I knew all about it. "I found the key," I said.

"You're a clever girl, Addie," he said, "but not quite clever enough! There is no key to that box, young lady. You've been lying. I don't believe you even have it."

"Oh, yes, I do!" I cried, without thinking far enough ahead. "But I've read the letter to Uncle Ben."

"What does it say?"

"Oh, it tells why you left home. And about the money." Another wild guess.

"Well, what are you going to do about it?"

"Nothing," I said. "Positively nothing. I promise!"

"You'd better not. It would hurt several people you love." Louis was looking at me as though he expected me to challenge that.

I took another chance. "Are you and Eliza about to do the same thing you did before?" I asked.

That was one question too many—Louis' words came out in a strangled way. "If you try to ruin my plans, young lady. I'll—I'll go to any lengths to stop you! Do you understand that?"

"Oh yes, Louis! I understand!"

"I want you to turn over the box and the letter immediately. You haven't shown it to anyone, have you?"

"Oh no! I haven't! I promise!" I couldn't think of a way to get out of the whole lie.

"I want you to *swear* to me right now that you will never tell a soul about it. For Tom's sake. Think what it would do to him. How ashamed he'd be. You wouldn't want that, would you?"

"Oh no! Honest, I wouldn't. I promise not to tell!"

"*Swear* on the soul of your Aunt Eveline! That if you ever tell—her soul will be damned!"

"Oh, I couldn't do that!" I cried in horror. "I *promise*

I won't tell but—"

"A promise is not enough. If you swear before God on her soul, I know you'll keep quiet. Swear!"

"I swear."

"Say the whole thing—I, Adelaide Agnew do swear—before God—"

"I, Addie, do swear before God that if I ever tell," I choked on the words, "Aunt Eveline's soul will be—will be damned!"

"You have taken an oath now, Addie. Do you know what that means?" Without waiting for an answer, he said, "It means that you have made a serious, solemn vow before God as binding as a marriage vow. You must stick to it, or your soul will be damned along with your aunt's. You will both burn forever in the fire of hell!" At that precise moment I fell head over heels out of love. How could I ever have thought he was good-looking? I hated his looks.

"The minute we get out of this house, I want that box and that letter," he repeated. "I mean that."

"All right," I said quietly. Then, suddenly, like clouds opening up to reveal the sun, his whole face changed, and he smiled in his old charming way.

"There, Addie! I'm sure we're such good friends that this little misunderstanding can't come between us." But it was too late for even friendship between us.

I went down the steps on shaky legs, and Louis came

right behind me.

By the time we got to the street, I had it figured out. "Look, Louis," I said, "you know I'm not going to tell anyone because I have made a solemn vow on Aunt Eveline's soul. I'd give you the box, but the truth is I hid it at Aunt Toosie's, and I can't get it back so easily. It's at the top of Aunt Toosie's closet, you see."

"I don't believe you," Louis said.

"I promise!" I turned on my most sincere look and crossed my fingers. "I *had* to hide it there, because it was the only place I could think of where Sandra Lee wouldn't find it. Aunt Toosie's closet is a mess. She *never* cleans it out! I'll have to wait, of course," I continued, trying harder for the sincere look. "Uncle Henry and Sandra Lee will have to be out, too. So I can't tell exactly when but meanwhile I swear I won't tell. On Aunt Eveline's s-soul! I swear."

"That's just not enough, young lady!" he said. "I'll give you the rest of the day, and that's all. I expect to have that box and that letter in my hand before I go to sleep tonight. Do you understand?"

"Oh yes, Louis! I'll get it! I'm sure I can get it before then!"

"I'm sure, too." Louis gave me such a look I started running. Ahead of me, I saw Nini coming down the street on her way to Tom's. Good, safe Nini! I looked over my shoulder to see if Louis was coming, but he watched me stop and wait for Nini, and then he turned and went inside.

"I see you're acting like twenty going on thirty," was Nini's cold greeting.

"Oh, Nini, don't be mad," I said. "I need you. You're just who I want to see."

"Why you buttering me up? What are you after now?" Nini asked.

"Nini, you know I love you—why are you being so mean to me?"

"Now, child, I'm not being mean to you! What's troubling you?" She was melting. "I love you too, Addie, and it's that what tears me up when I see you making a fool of yourself. That man, child! That man. You get sweet eyes when you look at him like you think he's a boy your age. He's *old*, Addie, and he's led himself a mean life! He left his wife and a baby!"

"I know all that. And I do not get sweet eyes, as you put it, over any man. Especially that one. I don't even like him. So there!"

"Well, Addie, I'm mighty glad to hear it. Mighty glad. What can I do for you?"

"Tell me everything you know!" I said promptly. "Where's the Japanese box that used to be on Aunt Eveline's dresser? What did Louis do besides leave Tom and Aunt Mabel? He *must* have done something else! What else did he do that's so bad, and how am I mixed up in it?"

"Whew, I'll be standing here a month answering that quiz!"

"Quit stalling, Nini. Tell me everything. I've got to know!"

"Oh, my," said Nini. "Oh, my, please let me be doing the right thing!" she said. "Addie, the secret's in that old box that used to sit on your aunt's dresser all right! 'Nini,' she told me, 'when I die, see that Addie gets this box, but not till she has some sense. She's too young to figure it all out now, but it's her right to know the secret of this box some day.' Yes, Addie, those were her very words!"

"Well, where is it?" I asked.

"Ah, there's the problem," said Nini. "I never knew exactly what your Aunt Eveline meant, but she hinted it had to do with that man and with you and Three Twenty. There never was anything in the box, but she told me you'd puzzle it out when the time came."

"There was a letter in it," I said.

"No, there wasn't," Nini answered. "Another difficulty," said Nini. "When your aunt died and they gave everything away, I put the box in the Great Catch-all for safe keeping. I figured your Aunt Toosie'd find it and know what to do, but she left it. Then, last time I came to pinch-hit for Tom's family and that man had come home, I thought it might be time for you to puzzle out your secret." Nini paused.

"So the box was there all along, and you finally decided I had enough sense?!" I asked sarcastically.

"Another problem," said Nini. "I decided you had no sense when I saw you making a food of yourself over a married man, so I decided to take the box back to my house."

"Well, give it to me now, Nini, or Aunt Eveline will go to hell and so will I maybe a lot sooner than you think too! Can I have it? Please?!"

"No, child," said Nini simply. "When I went to get it in the Great Catch-all, it wasn't there."

"Then I'd better disappear for good," I said. "If I don't give Louis the box and the letter tonight, he'll kill me!"

Twelve

"You mean he hasn't even committed—it—with Eliza?!" Sandra Lee stood with a soapy dish in her hand.

"No, I think he's too old for adultery," I whispered, waiting for her to rinse so that I could dry.

We were doing the dinner dishes and talking low, even though Aunt Toosie and Uncle Henry were in the living room laughing loudly at Fred Allen's jokes about Jack Benny on the radio. "You've *got* to help me find that box!"

"He might try to kill you because you know too much! Even though he loves you!" Sandra Lee continued, letting the hot water run. "How romantic!"

"There is nothing romantic about being dead," I said dryly. I had had enough of impressing Sandra Lee; I just wanted to find the box.

"He is a passionate man!" Sandra Lee sighed. "I can tell by the way he looks at you."

Yesterday I would have loved the tone of envy in her voice, but there were more pressing matters at the moment. "I've got to find the box *tonight*!" I said urgently. "Uncle Malvern is my only hope. He could have found it that time in the attic. I'm going to search his room!"

"I'm coming with you!" said Sandra Lee. "You can pretend you came to talk to Uncle Malvern about his machine, and while you keep him occupied, I can look through his room."

As usual, Sandra Lee had maneuvered herself into the most interesting part of a scheme, but this time I didn't care, as long as she helped me.

We hung up the dish towels and turned off the light. It was dark outside, and I wondered whether Louis was waiting for me in the shadows. I stuck close to Sandra Lee, and was happy when we shut Aunt Mabel's door behind us and stood in her cozy kitchen.

"Oh, Uncle Malvern," Sandra Lee said, "I'm so glad you're home! I wanted you to tell Addie all about your trip in the Time Machine!" He was sitting at the kitchen table, a glass of beer in his hand.

Aunt Mabel rolled her eyes to heaven and turned back to washing dishes. I sat down next to Uncle Malvern and put a listening look on my face while Sandra Lee sneaked up the back steps to Uncle Malvern's room.

"Well, Addie," said Uncle Malvern. "I know you think I'm off my rocker a bit. No, no, don't interrupt. I know what everyone thinks of me, and I don't mind! Well, it isn't that I don't mind, but I'm used to it."

"Please, Uncle Malvern, Tom doesn't think you're crazy and—neither do I."

"Tom's a great lad," said Uncle Malvern, his red eyes filling. "You're great too, Addie. The truth is, I really stumbled into something with my Time Machine. It works! Maybe not as well as Jules Verne's, but I have succeeded in going back to my youth! When I get in the Time Machine, what with one thing and another I've set up, old photographs and the like, I am in the past again, seeing it with new eyes!"

I was trying hard to listen, but his speech was blurry and I was wondering where Louis was and what Sandra Lee was finding. Aunt Mabel dried her hands and went through the swinging door to the living room.

"I am there," Uncle Malvern said, "reliving past events, only this time I'm there with knowledge of the future, if you get my meaning. I was in the Machine the other day, and I traveled back to a time before you were born when all of us young people, your mother, Eveline, Ben, Louis, and I, had been invited to a wedding. It was the wedding of Norma Jean's parents and it took place at Oakwood! At the reception, Louis came up to me and said, 'Dance with my little cousin Eliza, Malvern—she's only sixteen, and she's standing there all alone at the edge of the dance floor, looking at the wedding couple and wishing she were the bride! An older man like yourself will give her a thrill!'"

Uncle Malvern had all of my attention.

"I danced with Eliza, but I'm afraid I didn't give her

a thrill. I only had eyes for your mother, and Eliza never took her eyes off Simeon Valerie dancing with his bride. Yes, the new Mrs. has had a crush on her hubby all this time! Yes, indeedy."

"Did you see anything else in the Time Machine, Uncle Malvern?" I asked. "Another time?" I added encouragingly.

Uncle Malvern looked at me through half-closed eyes. "As a matter of fact, I did. I was riding along, and I saw you when you were a little girl. Eveline and taken Tom and you to the park earlier, and I had come over to Three Twenty to get Tom. It was right after your Uncle Ben's death, and your Aunt Eveline was still going through his things. Well, sir, I didn't intend to snoop, but I saw a letter. Just the envelope. It was addressed to Ben in Louis' handwriting, and your Aunt Eveline was standing by the window, a little box in one hand and the letter in the other. She looked stricken, and she murmured. 'Addie, oh Addie!'"

"Why was she saying my name?" I asked.

"I'm not sure! I thought I saw her put the letter back in the box. I got a good look—it was the little Japanese box that later she always kept on her dresser." Uncle Malvern hung his head and his voice faded.

"Did you find the box in the Great Catch-all that night?" I asked, holding my breath for an answer.

"Yes."

"Where is it?!"

Uncle Malvern was staring at me, his mouth open, his eyes blurring.

"It's back in the past, Addie," he said, his words starting to blend together, "but I'm afraid the letter is lost in time." And with that, his head nodded, and he fell asleep.

"It's not anywhere," Sandra Lee tiptoed up and whispered. "I looked all through his armoire."

"I'm going to look now," I whispered back. "You stay with Uncle Malvern," and before she could object I ran up the back stairs. I sneaked past Tom's dark room and tiptoed without a sound past the lighted guest room where Louis was staying. I could hear him typing something, but I had to take a chance and I didn't have much to lose. I crept down the hall.

Uncle Malvern's room was lit by an oil lamp and looked eerie; the lamp cast a weird, dull glow and made tall shadows on Uncle Malvern's crazy contraption. The Time Machine was a maze of chains, wooden crates, pipes, my easel, Aunt Mabel's discarded foot-pedal sewing machine, and, in the center at the top, Tom's old bicycle. Thumb-tacked to the wall were old snapshots and souvenirs of Uncle Malvern's youth. It was all linked together in a kind of ingenious way, like Uncle Malvern himself, a jumble of intelligent ideas forming a crazy, useless whole.

The only other things in the room were a bed crowded against the wall, and an armoire much smaller than the Great Catch-all. The armoire was neat as a pin: on the hanging side there were four suits, two sweaters, and a coat; on the shelf side, I could see at a glance there was nothing except neatly folded underwear, two hats, handkerchiefs, and shirts, ironed to perfection by Aunt Mabel.

I climbed the stepladder that led to the bicycle seat and sat down. I put my feet on the pedals and began to ride. The room came alive: wheels turned, water poured out of a pipe and flowed onto a small paddle wheel in a pail, and the paddle wheel turned, pushing the water over the edge into a larger tub before piping it back. The handle of Tom's old phonograph dropped to a record and scratched out the sad strains of "There's A Long Long Trail A-Winding."

The oil lamp made the shadow jump, shrink, and grow rhythmically to the sound of the tiny waterfall and the melancholy music. I really felt as though I were moving; I was traveling back in time on Uncle Malvern's machine through the changing shadow, back over the years, looking for a Japanese box with a letter inside.

Directly in front of me and tacked to the wall was a wilted blossom of magnolia fuscata that smelled like banana oil. Under it was a snapshot of Aunt Eveline. She was standing in a garden, wearing a wide-brimmed hat that shaded part of her face, so that I couldn't see her eyes. Her mouth was slightly open as though she were saying,

"Look around you, Addie, and you'll find the box. Look carefully, Addie. I mean for you to have it, but don't act hastily, now. Think long and hard, Addie. There it is!"

And there it was. I saw the Japanese box on top of the armoire, too high to see if you were standing on the floor.

I reached out and grabbed it. I was back in the present, so excited and curious my hands were shaking. The box was as pretty as I remembered. It was made of light wood with a picture painted on the lid. The picture was of a landscape with a person standing under a tree, looking at a snow-capped mountain in the background. I opened the box. It was empty. I turned it over in my hand, but there was nothing on the back except "Made in Japan."

"But there's nothing in it!" I said aloud.

"So, you haven't read the letter after all! You've never even seen it!" Louis said. "I've been waiting for you!"

I jumped, lost my balance, and almost fell. He was blocking the doorway, and the look on his face told me he was ready to go to any lengths.

"Hand over the box, Addie." Louis moved forward and put his foot on the first step of the Time Machine.

There are moments when I'm glad I haven't turned into a lady yet. I can still move and think like a child, and that's what I did. Quick as a jackrabbit, I started the Time Machine. I pedaled as fast as I could, and when the whole machine was trembling with speed, just as Louis reached out for me, I ducked under his arm, made a gigantic leap to the floor, and tore down the hall. Behind me, I heard a thundering crash, and knew Louis had fallen into all those pipes and wheels and wrecked Uncle Malvern's Time Machine.

I took the short cut through the back yard of Three Twenty and raced to my room. Clutched in my hand was the box. I heard the front door slam, but, thank goodness, it was Sandra Lee's footsteps dashing up the stairs. She burst into my room.

"Did you find it?" she said.

What made me lie? I don't know. "No," I answered.

"Boy, was that a mess!" Sandra Lee said. "When I got there, Louis was draped over your old easel, rubbing his shin. He'd knocked the needle on the record of 'The Music Goes Round and Round' and it was stuck on 'round and round'!" Sandra Lee laughed happily. "He didn't look so glamorous after all! The crash was so loud, even Uncle Malvern woke up, and he's up there crying over his machine!"

"I guess it's wrecked forever," I said.

"You should have seen it! Louis cursing, Aunt Mabel fussing, and Uncle Malvern wringing his hands. It was a scream!"

"Ha, ha," I said weakly.

"Maybe the box is still in the Great Catch-all," Sandra Lee said. "You look. I'm sick of Louis."

When Sandra Lee closed her door, the house became quiet. Outside, I heard the sound of rustling leaves. Afraid to look, I wondered what I'd do if it was Louis under my window. I knew it was the letter he wanted that had once been in the box. Now, he knew it wasn't there and I hadn't read it. There was no reason to come after me, was there? I lay in the dark, trying to calm down, and turning the box in my hand. Suddenly, I felt a rough place. I turned on my bed lamp and propped myself on my elbow to examine the box more carefully. There was a seam in the wood on one side, where I'd felt the edge, and the seam had a tiny hole in it. I took a pin and touched the hole with the point. It was like magic: immediately, part of the side slid back and revealed a secret panel that hid a tiny hollow space between the inside bottom of the box and the outside bottom. There was a thin, yellowing envelope hidden there. I pulled it out and opened it up. Inside it was a letter written to my Uncle Ben and signed by Louis.

The letter was dated September 29, 1928 and read:

> Dear Ben,
> By the time you read this I'll be far away, but I
> want you to know that I'm not running out on you.

This letter is an I.O.U.

Ben, in the beginning, I honestly thought I'd strike it rich and pay you back double, just as I'd promised. Then, when we got to 200 feet, I saw the whole structure of the earth was wrong and that the reservoir of oil was further to the west, much nearer Oakwood than my cousin Eliza's place at Burnside.

Ben, I'm damn sorry! But I made an honest mistake! I felt so bad about the $5,000 you'd lent me and of course, I wanted to pay you back so, Ben, I lied to you. Yes, I told you I knew the oil was at 500 feet and that I needed $5,000 more to drill deeper.

The truth is, I just couldn't figure any other way to pay you back without borrowing more. But if I could get my hands on another $5,000 I knew how to double it. You see, there was this guy out at the Fairgrounds who'd been giving Eliza tips and he'd just told her about an absolutely sure thing: he knew the owners of this horse and he knew they themselves were betting everything they had on him. I could win back your $5,000 and then some! I made the plunge, confident and happy. Three quarters round the track when that horse was a length ahead and going strong, he pulled up suddenly and almost stopped. They found out later there was a nail left on the track when they'd constructed the infield—it had gone clean into the horse's hoof. Who could have *guessed that fine animal would break down and not even finish the race?!*

Ben, I can't stay in this two-bit job at the Exploration Company and make enough to repay you and support Mabel and my baby as well, but I have an opportunity in another state—yes, sir, Ben, this time I'm positive there's oil, and I'm going to make a fortune! I wish I could tell you more, because I know I could ease your mind. Just let me say this: you'll be able to pay off the mortgage you had to take out on Three Twenty Audubon Street when you lent me the money. This time, I won't fail you!

Now, I have to ask you the hard part: Ben, don't tell anyone! I tried to think of a way to explain it all to Mabel, but I've decided it's best to disappear and do the explaining when I come home again. Mabel would never see it my way—meanwhile, Malvern will take care of her and my baby.

Ben, thank you for everything you've done and all the things I know you'll do. Keep this letter in this little Japanese box and Eveline'll never find it. I'll make it good to you before you know it—you'll get every cent of your $10,000 back.

Yours,

Louis.

That letter explained a million things at once. I knew why Louis had run off, and how I was involved. The money had never been paid back, and Louis owed it to me!

Aunt Eveline must have found out after Uncle Ben died and she went through his things. She hadn't told anyone except Nini.

"Nini," Aunt Eveline must have said, "there's something I want to tell you, and you must keep it secret. Louis Martin is a thief and the person he's robbed is Addie. Because of him, there's a heavy mortgage on our house. I've kept up the payment by the hardest work, but I won't be here much longer—now, Nini, please don't interrupt with false hopes; the Lord is calling me and that's that. Toosie will have to sell Three Twenty to pay off the mortgage and there'll be nothing left for Addie's education.

"Her only hope is in this box. There's no sense revealing all of this now—it wouldn't help Addie and would destroy Mabel and Tom. But if Louis ever comes back, which I seriously doubt, and Addie's old enough to handle the situation, I want you to give this box to her."

Louis must have failed another time, and now he was planning to do it all over again, and it was the Valeries he'd swindle. Norma Jean would lose Oakwood just like I'd lost Three Twenty Audubon Street!

Thirteen

I lay in bed, staring at the flowered wallpaper. There was every reason for Louis to come after me. The glass wind chimes in my window hung like chiseled slits in solid air. It was as still and quiet as Aunt Eveline's tomb. Out of the corner of my eye, I saw a shadow near the curtain bulge and change shape.

"Now," said Aunt Eveline. Her presence was as real to me as the hand I stretched out toward her. "The time has come."

"For what?" I mumbled.

"To grow up. To act. To do the right thing."

"There are shadings of right and wrong, Aunt Eveline," I whispered. "Everything is not black and white. Some things are gray."

"There is a passage in Revelations that says, 'Because you are neither hot nor cold, because you are lukewarm, I will spit you out of my mouth!'"

"But Louis may kill me if I don't hand over the letter." Silence. "On the other hand, he owes me the money, and I want to go to Art School."

"You could work your way through college if, after all

of this boy-craziness, there's really anything left of your burning ambition to be an artist," came the answer.

"Of course, I want to be an artist more than anything!"

"Your actions belie your words, my girl. And—if you tell anyone about this letter, you will create a scandal that will humiliate Tom, to say nothing of his mother. Who knows—there may be oil this time. Or, if the hole turns up dry, it still doesn't mean Louis will run off again owing money. Louis started out with Ben in good faith. Besides, he claims to have mended his ways."

"I don't believe him. He has a silver tongue."

"You believed him when you wanted to."

"But now, I really think he might—he might go to any lengths!"

"What does that mean?"

"He might commit the fifth commandment instead of the sixth."

"Nonsense, he won't kill you."

"If I don't tell Mr. Valerie, he might mortgage Oakwood like Uncle Ben did Three Twenty, and then Norma Jean would lose Oakwood for good."

"Mr. Valerie is a grown man, capable of making his own decisions."

"And what about your soul, Aunt Eveline?"

"My soul has nothing to do with you. That promise had no meaning except to intimidate you. Get on with your thinking."

"I don't know what to do. Am I supposed to just give Louis $10,000 that is rightfully mine and let him try to swindle Mr. Valerie?"

"Think about it, Addie! I waited until I thought you were grown up enough to handle all of this. Are you?" And with that, Aunt Eveline swept out of my mind.

I did think about it. I thought about how being grown-up had two parts, and the part Aunt Eveline was interested in had nothing to do with hips and curves. It was all mind and straight lines, and not much fun. It was like walking along a good road that kept branching off in thorny paths, and you had to take the thorny paths instead of the comfortable road to get to Grown-up.

I knew that I should do all right. For one thing, I hadn't even heard about the money until now, but it had never occurred to me that I wouldn't be able to go to art school. Aunt Toosie would see to that and, even if it meant I had to get a small job on the side, that wasn't the end of the world. I didn't really need $10,000.

Then, I tried to imagine what it would be like for Tom if he knew his father was a crook. I was sure Tom would think it was the worst possible thing that could be true, and he'd have to live with it always.

No, there was no gray about what I had to do: I had to make Louis go back to the Salvation Army by telling him I'd show everyone the letter if he didn't. Then after he left, I'd have to tear up the letter and never, never tell a living soul.

All right, then. I would prove I was mature by giving up the money and keeping my mouth shut.

I snuggled down under my covers, my conscience clear, my mind made up about everything black, white, and even gray. I thought about how great it is to think things through before you act, and I made up my mind never never to act without thinking again. I would renounce men and concentrate on my art. I would work my way through college. I felt wonderful.

It was midnight when I heard a pebble hit my screen. He was out there! He was right under my window, ready to climb in, his feet on Aunt Toosie's rose trellis, his hands reaching up to my window sill, then the top of his head, his angry eyes... I squealed, jumped out of bed, and backed up against the wall. Another pebble hit the screen.

"Addie!" Slowly, it seemed against my will, I tiptoed to the window and made myself look down. Louis was standing below balancing on crutches and looking up.

"Come down and bring the box. Now!" he said just loud enough for me to hear.

My mind went blank. I felt as trapped as if he'd been in my room gripping my arm. Everything I'd thought out so carefully was mixed up in a blur of fear. Like a zombie, I slipped on the dress I'd thrown on a chair, and with the letter in my pocket and the box in my hand,

I crept through the dark, quiet house and out the back door to the yard.

I walked slowly to the side under my window. Louis hobbled out of the shadows. He was bent over, balancing on crutches that I recognized as the ones Tom had used when he broke his leg last year. They were too short for Louis, and made him look like a very old man. He reached out and I handed him the box without even realizing it.

Louis opened the secret panel. "I want the letter!" he said angrily, glaring at me. "Give it to me!" Then he remembered, and turned sweet again. "You don't understand, Addie. This time there really is oil. I'm positive! I can pay you back, too!"

"I don't want the money," I said, everything suddenly clear again, "but if you go back to the Salvation Army, I'll tear up the letter and I swear I'll never tell Tom or anyone."

Louis laughed in an ugly way. "You can't threaten me. You're a child. And you've already sworn on your aunt's soul!"

"That doesn't count, and if you stay, I'll show Mr. Valerie the letter. They'll believe the letter!" I said, pulling it out of my pocket and shaking it at him.

"Give me that letter, Addie!" Louis hobbled toward me. "I mean to have it." He moved nearer to me.

"It won't do you any good," I said, backing up,

"because I made a copy and Sandra Lee has it. She knows everything and if something happened to me, or this letter, she'll give the copy to Aunt Toosie and Aunt Toosie..." Louis was not listening. He hadn't seemed to hear a thing after I said the letter had been copied. His face was contorted into a mask of iron rage, and he lunged at me, lost his balance, and fell to his knees in the ridiculous pose of an old-fashioned marriage proposal. "Will you marry me, Dolores darling?" I thought, and laughed hysterically. I jumped out of his reach just as he grabbed me again.

"You can trust me never to tell!" I cried. "I promise! Aunt Eveline kept the secret for Aunt Mabel and I'm doing it for Tom! I just made that up about Sandra Lee having a copy." I watched his face change.

"Look," I said holding up the letter as though I were going to tear it. "If you really love Tom, swear to me on your soul that you'll forget about Oakwood and go back to the Salvation Arm,y and I'll tear up the letter right now!"

"How do I know you'll keep your word and not tell?" he asked.

"I'll swear on Aunt Eveline's soul *and* mine! If you swear, too."

He sighed.

"Swear," I said.

"I do," he said solemnly, as in a marriage vow.

"Now tear up the letter, please." I tore it in half, and then into small pieces, while Louis watched. "You win, Addie," he said with all of his old charm. "You're a very special young lady in my book, Addie, dear!"

As he turned and hobbled away, I thought of how much "young lady" and a "dear" after my name would have meant to me once. Now, I only thought of how good it would be to get in my new Early American bed and go to sleep.

Fourteen

"Wake up, Addie!" Uncle Henry called. "I smell bacon and eggs!" I jumped out of bed and rushed to the window. The sycamores that shade our street in the summer were bare of their wide leaves, and a cold wind was rustling them, dry and brown, down the sidewalk.

I could see all the way to the corner. The street looked empty because Louis' car was gone. It was all over—a whole stage of my life.

I had loved loving Louis. It had been a real romance with excitement, mystery, and unexpected things happening. Maybe some of it had been make-believe in a way, and in another way, deep down, I had hoped Louis would love Aunt Mabel again so that Tom could have a father, but now I was back to my ho-hum life, where the most important things were how to survive Junior Debs and how to turn the play into something better than a crushing bore and—oh yes, I'd almost forgotten my burning ambition—how to become a famous artist.

With Louis back at the Salvation Army and my mouth shut, Tom would never know his father was a thief and Norma Jean wouldn't lose Oakwood; I'd sacrificed

$10,000 for others. The only trouble was, no one knew how good I was.

Sandra Lee stuck her head in my door. "Breakfast!" she said. She opened the door wider and stopped, staring at me. "You look different."

"I have broken up with Louis," I said.

Sandra Lee drew in her breath in a slight gasp, and then said, "At least, you'll have the fun of trying to get someone else."

"I've given up all that sort of thing," I said grandly.

Sandra Lee didn't answer for a minute. "Well, it is a lot of work trying to be adorable all the time," she said. "We're going to be late for school."

Sandra Lee looked thoughtful as she munched her corn flakes. Hidden behind the newspaper, Uncle Henry ate his bacon and eggs, and Aunt Toosie talked non-stop as she walked back and forth from the kitchen, carrying plates and sipping her café au lait whenever she passed her place.

"There! You've got to be firm," said Uncle Henry interrupting her from behind the paper. "Listen to these headlines: 'Japanese Back Down in Pacific Crises! The enemy says, we will continue with sincerity to try to find a peaceful solution!' You see, Toosie, if Roosevelt wasn't tough in these talks, they'd be in California this minute!"

Sandra Lee rolled her eyes at me. "By the way, Addie," she said. "Did you borrow my Halo shampoo?"

"My God!" thundered Uncle Henry, slamming his paper on his knee, "Is it *possible*?!"

"Is what possible, dear?" Aunt Toosie asked mildly in a comforting tone.

"Yes, it is possible. In fact, probable, that when the Japanese sail up the Mississippi to occupy New Orleans, they will march up Audubon Street and find two young ladies shampooing their hair with no idea that we've LOST THE WAR!"

"Oh, Daddy," Sandra Lee said, "we're not even in that old stupid war!"

"We will be!" shouted Uncle Henry. "Pray God not too late!"

"Yes, dear, I agree," said Aunt Toosie, "and speaking of late, it's time to go, girls, and Addie, we'll have to ask Norma Jean over since you've spent the night there."

"Uh-huh," I answered. Why would Norma Jean want to come over here, when she had Oakwood?

"Why don't you invite her to spend the night next Saturday?"

"Er—ah."

"Mother," said Sandra Lee folding her napkin and standing up. "Don't worry about it. We'll pick up Norma Jean on the way to school. She doesn't want to spend the night here when she can go to Oakwood. And she'll think we've invited her so we can go, too. Come on, Addie. 'Bye, Daddy."

Uncle Henry allowed himself to be kissed. "Listen to this, Toosie," he said as we went out the door. "Roosevelt is cutting short his vacation in Warm Springs because Hull says…"

When we passed Three Twenty, Norma Jean wasn't in sight.

"We're late," I said impatiently. "Norma Jean is probably sick this morning, anyway." I started to walk on.

"Wait," Sandra Lee said. She ran up the walk, banged on the door, and yelled, "Hurry up, Norma Jean! You'll be late!"

The door flew open, and Eliza and Norma Jean stood there. Eliza smiled with relief at Sandra Lee and me and said, "There, Norma Jean, I told you Addie would pass by and you wouldn't have to go alone."

Of course, Aunt Eveline was present to point out to me the various lessons to be learned from the scene, such as how thoughtful Sandra Lee was, and why couldn't I think of anyone besides myself.

But when the three of us arrived at school, Sandra Lee immediately forgot her role as protector of Norma Jean; she had too much to do maintaining her own image as the cutest girl around. Still, I could see that Norma Jean's arrival under the wing of Sandra Lee had already had its effect. The great Betsy welcomed her like an old friend. Suddenly, it was "in" to be nice to Norma Jean. It was obviously better than medicine for Norma Jean.

By lunchtime, she had lost her pinched, scared look and seemed to be enjoying herself, in a quiet way.

In the cafeteria, we pushed our trays along, and Sandra Lee said to Norma Jean, loud enough for some of the other girls to hear, "There is a legend that just before Our Lady was taken up into heaven, she gave her secret recipes to this cafeteria. Unfortunately, us poor mortals cannot taste the heavenly part."

That brought the house down and further established Norma Jean. She sat down next to me.

"Louis left," I said, expecting to add to her happiness and cash in on some of her popularity.

"I know."

"Aren't you glad he's going back to the Salvation Army?"

"He's gone to Oakwood," Norma Jean said. "He left with my father. They've formed a company, and they'll start drilling for oil in a few weeks."

"Oh!" I wailed. "You'll lose Oakwood! He'll steal it from you just like he stole Three Twenty from me! Eliza changed the books so your father would think he needed money!"

I said all that without one thought for Norma Jean.

"My father knows what Eliza did," Norma Jean said. "She cried and told him everything right in front of me. He put his arms around her and made me come over to him and then he said, 'I have three loves: my wife, my daughter, and my home, and I intend to keep all three.' He said Louis may be right, and he can handle him in any case."

"Oh," I said.

I left my red beans and rice and stumbled out of the cafeteria. When the bell rang, my feet carried me to Religion class, but my mind was busy thinking about how I had completely forgotten my good intentions and how I had blurted out all those secrets to Norma Jean, and how, no matter what I planned to do, I always did the opposite. I sat down at my desk, hating myself and wondering if I would ever learn not to say the first thing that came into my head. Suddenly, I heard Sister Neeley say, "Some of you young ladies seem to think that it doesn't matter what you do, if you want to do it badly enough."

Did she know what I was thinking?! "Yes, she's got her eyes on you all right!" Aunt Eveline said it so loud I half-turned to see if anyone else had heard her.

I put an innocent, interested expression on my face. Sister Neeley continued, "Our Lady is your model. Not the skin-deep Cecil B. DeMille Mary with black hair." Pause. I felt the blood rushing to my face. I examined the inkwell on my desk, ran my finger along the indentation for pencils. "No," she said, "it doesn't matter what color Mary's hair was. It is her soul that counts. She was the first lady. Our Lady." Outside, a blue jay was fussing in the tree. I found my eyes glued to the top of my desk.

"Mary was compassionate and loving; she would never have acted for her own selfish gain. That is what being a lady means."

There was no way I could control my face as I felt myself being cast as the perfect non-lady of all times. I was a selfish child, the opposite of all the things Sister Neeley was talking about. I had already told Norma Jean something that could have hurt her, and now Tom would know that his father had been a thief. Oh, Aunt Eveline, why didn't you make a lady out of me when you had the chance?

I thought about how I'd always trampled over everyone in sight, including Norma Jean, Tom, Louis, Aunt Mabel, Sandra Lee, Nini, Pumpkin, Uncle Malvern and, Oh Lord, if I've left anyone out, please add them to the list before I go to confession so I can start out with a clean slate.

I felt better already. I would make amends. It was not too late. I could just see myself, my inner radiance shining through, touching my face with such beauty that even my nose looked shorter.

The new Addie heard the bell and stood up. In ladylike fashion, she gathered her books and walked with dignity into the hall.

"Hey, Addie!" shouted Sandra Lee, rushing up. "Can you take my books home? I promised Leonard I'd meet him at the drug store for a soda. Please, Addie?"

"Carry your own stupid books," I said.

"Gee, thanks," said Sandra Lee in hurt tones. "Are you going somewhere?"

"I'm going to hell," I said, busting into tears. "I'll never be a lady!"

"A lady? What are you talking about? For goodness sakes, you didn't take all that lady-stuff seriously did you? Stop being a crybaby! Do you want to come with me?"

"And let Leonard think I'm tagging along with you just to see him? No, thank you. Here, give me your books. I'm going home and then I'm going to Tom's. I can take your books."

More tears caught me by surprise on the way home. I felt worse than I'd felt since the day of Aunt Eveline's funeral. I missed her. I would always miss her, and I'd never get used to it. I had no one to love, and no one loved me. At least not like Aunt Eveline had. I was crying hard as I ran up the stairs to my room.

"Tom!" I wailed aloud without meaning to. It was because I could be myself with Tom, and I didn't have to say the right thing or bat my eyelashes or do any of the things advised in *Dearest*. Tom didn't care, because he loved me. Oh, Tom, I'm so sorry I told Norma Jean your father is a thief! I'll make her promise not to tell anyone. Suddenly, I thought, did I love him? I mean, was I in love with Tom after all these years? I was so surprised, I stopped crying to figure it out.

I forgot I had given up men forever. I tackled my hair with the curling iron—just a little. I made the ends curl under in a pageboy and push my bangs to one side so that my right eye was covered like Veronica Lake's. Sandra Lee had some pancake make-up that made your skin look pale and smooth, and I borrowed some of that along with a dot of her dime-store perfume, "Temptress," behind each ear. I told Aunt Toosie I had cramps and didn't want dinner. I waited until the kitchen light went out and I heard the radio in the living room. I was ready to fill in the blanks on page 96.

I sneaked out through the dark kitchen, taking care that no one saw me. On the other side of Three Twenty, I could see a light. It was a school night, and Tom was in his room studying. I walked quietly, trying not to crunch the dry leaves on the ground, and stage-whispered under his window. "Tom!" I tried to make my voice exciting but it's hard with a one-syllable name. You can kind of sing Leon-ard and Lou-is, but what can you do with Tom?

"What? I can't hear you," he yelled back.

"Come down," I called.

He pulled on a sweater as he climbed out the window and down through the tree. "What's the matter?" he asked, looking worried.

"Nothing," I said. "Nothing important."

"I thought something had happened to Pumpkin!" He sighed with relief.

That seemed a poor beginning. How was he going to notice my smooth shining hair and silky skin if he was thinking about his dog? I tried again.

"Tom, let's go for a walk."

"At this time of night?! Where do you have to go?"

"I don't have to go anywhere, Tom. I just thought it would be nice to walk in the moonlight."

"There's no moon tonight, Addie. What's wrong with you? You look pale—God. I didn't notice! You look awful! Are you sick?"

"I am not sick, Tom. I am fine. I just wanted to be with you," I'd said it. Light was dawning on his face.

"You did?" He was looking at me so intently I felt myself blush and lowered my eyes.

"Let's take a walk," he said, taking my hand but not moving. He was still looking at me. For the first time in my life, I was tongue-tied with Tom. I could feel my blood racing, but my mouth wouldn't open, and my mind had shut down. He was definitely not thinking about Pumpkin.

"Addie," he said. It was much nicer than Leonard's Ad-die. He put his hand under my chin and lifted my face, pulling me toward him. I knew I was supposed to close my eyes, but I didn't want to miss anything.

"I love you, Addie," he said.

I wanted to say, "I love you, too, Tom," but he was kissing me and I couldn't. Suddenly the kitchen door to

Tom's house opened, and light flooded the yard and us.

"Tom!? Is that you?" Aunt Mabel was standing in the kitchen door. She couldn't miss us. "Addie!" Her voice was full of shock. Suddenly all the beauty of the moment was gone, and I felt ashamed. Nice girls did not kiss boys late at night in the dark. If she hadn't appeared, I might even have gone too far!

"Tom, what are you doing out there?" Aunt Mabel sounded like she was talking to Louis and she'd caught him stealing. She knew what Tom was doing.

"I'm taking Addie home," he said in tones that added "mind your business." "Come on, Addie, we'll walk around the block first."

"No—er no!" I said loud enough for Aunt Mabel to hear. "I have to study. I just came to ask you something about Latin verbs."

"Don't lie!" he whispered. "It doesn't matter what she thinks."

But it did. It did to me. I was tied in knots; no longer interested in kissing, much less going too far. "Goodnight, Tom" I said. "Thanks for your help!"

"No, wait, Addie!" Tom said. "I have to talk to you." He pulled me along to the front yard.

"Er—what do you want to talk about?" I said. Aunt Mabel was still standing in the doorway.

"Goodnight, Mother!" Tom called purposefully. "Let's really take a walk and I'll tell you."

It had turned chilly and I was shivering. Tom put his arm around my shoulders as we walked. It was different from the way he'd held me close when he kissed me.

"I've known something about my father for a long time," he said.

"You have!?" I stopped dead in my tracks. "What have you known?"

"I've known that he borrowed money from your Uncle Ben and never paid it back. And he did the same thing in Texas and got caught. He's been in jail, Addie. I don't know where he got that uniform either. He may have been in that New York settlement house, but he's not an officer in the Salvation Army."

"Tom!" I was so surprised I couldn't think. "How did you find out?"

"Do you remember the day we first found Pumpkin? I went over to your house to ask your Aunt Eveline if we could keep her. She was up in her room, and she didn't see me come in. She was holding the Japanese box and I could see a secret panel open. It looked so fascinating that I went back later to play with it. There was a letter in it from my father to your uncle. I read the letter. Then, just before I went off to school, a letter came from his probation officer. It was addressed in care of my mother but when I saw 'County Jail, Amarillo' on the envelope, I opened it and hid it from her."

"Why didn't you tell me?!"

"Addie, he's my *father*! And—and I think he's trying to change. He's a good geologist, you know; he only missed the oil by a little that time with your Uncle Ben. He doesn't mean to be dishonest. He's just—weak—and—he's my father." Tom stopped and looked at me so openly, I had to turn my eyes away.

"He and Mr. Valerie..." I began. "I found out about him too. I wasn't going to tell and then..."

"It doesn't matter," Tom interrupted. "This time he's formed a company. He's not borrowing from Mr. Valerie. I really think there is oil at Oakwood—everyone says so, and if he strikes it, he'll never have to borrow money again and he can stay home with my mother."

"But, Tom, I thought you hated your father!"

"I—I don't know how I feel. Remember that day at lunch you said, 'How else can he make up for all those years if they won't forgive you to begin with?'. Well, I think he's trying to change, and my mother won't give him a chance."

"But why didn't you tell me before?" I asked. "Didn't you trust me? We were supposed to be friends."

"You always act like I'm the only person you're not friends with. How am I supposed to believe you even like me, when you kick me around all the time?"

"I don't do that!"

"You give a good imitation. You can't even find a dance for me at Junior Debs, and you make me play

Joseph in your stupid dumb play!"

"That's an honor!"

"Addie, you know darn well you did it to be mean."

"Well, if I did, it was only because I cared. If I hadn't liked you, I wouldn't have been mean, even if I didn't know it."

"I'm not sure I follow that," Tom said and burst out laughing. "Come on, Addie, I'll walk you home. If I stay up any later, I'll be tired for practice tomorrow."

"You mean rehearsal," I said, knowing he didn't.

"I mean football," he said smiling at me.

Fifteen

It was a strange week. It didn't seem possible that I hadn't always been in love with Tom, and, with Louis gone, it was as though he'd never been around. Uncle Malvern was busy repairing the Time Machine, and Aunt Mabel was baking in a one-man marathon. She looked happy for a change, humming along as she bustled around the kitchen. Tom was trying to convince her that his father wanted to make up for what he'd done. Aunt Mabel's hair looked softer around her face, and I wondered if Tom was making headway, or if it was the heat from the oven that made little curls escape Aunt Mabel's French knot and frame her rosy cheeks.

But the play was still lifeless. Even with the gestures and shorter lines, it was discouragingly like it had always been—bad. I hardly saw Tom. He missed every rehearsal practicing for the last, biggest game of the season to be played Saturday morning. When he showed up Saturday afternoon for the dress rehearsal, he had a black eye, a swollen knee, and a mean look. This time I had watched, and Jesuit had lost; Tom had missed a pass in the end zone. He growled his lines in a sullen monotone and frowned at everyone on the stage.

"Joseph!" called Sister Maurice from the audience, "try not to limp! Put a little life into your lines, and cut the top off that Mardi Gras mask before you come tomorrow. The beard is disguise enough." Tom was wearing a mask that had belonged to Uncle Ben and had been stored in the Great Catch-all.

But no matter how we tried, dress rehearsal was terrible.

"That's supposed to mean the real play will go well," said Sandra Lee.

"That has not been my experience," said Sister Maurice, dryly. "Don't be late. Curtain's tomorrow at three sharp!"

The next day started just like any other Sunday, with mass and late breakfast.

Sandra Lee didn't seem nervous about her part in the play. Aunt Toosie sewed on her shimmering wings and ironed my blue cape.

"Your hair is a lovely length, Addie," she said. "You're growing up into such a pretty young lady! How I wish Eveline could see you!"

Sandra Lee and I left the house at two and stopped by for Norma Jean. She didn't seem nervous either, and she didn't look sick anymore, though she was still much too thin.

We walked down the block to the Convent, and

Sandra Lee and Norma Jean went inside to help Sister Maurice carry over some last-minute Realism in the form of fresh-cut palms.

From half a block away, I heard Tom yell, "Addie! I can't be in the play!"

"What?!" I yelled back. "What are you talking about?! The play goes on in an hour! There can't be a play without Joseph!"

He came panting up and said, "Find another Joseph, or pretend he's just offstage like you do with the camels. Addie, this is war! Pearl Harbor's been attacked!"

"Pearl Harbor? I don't know what you're talking about. What's Pearl Harbor?"

"It's a place! In Hawaii. It's where the U.S. fleet is— was, I don't know. The Japanese have bombed our fleet in a surprise attack! We're in it now for sure!"

"You don't have to sound so glad! What's so good about war?"

"I'm not glad, but it had to come. The only way we can beat Hitler is to go to war."

The United States at war? Us in a war? It didn't seem real. The play was real. Joseph was real. Tom was letting me down.

"I still fail to see the connection between Pearl Harbor and the role of Joseph," I said coldly.

"You don't actually expect me to act in a stupid play on the day my country is attacked, do you?!" he asked.

"Of course I do!" He'd called it a stupid play! "It doesn't affect you."

"Doesn't affect me?! Addie, you're dumb! I have to enlist. I haven't got time to think about a dumb play." Enlist? Go to war?

"You're too young!" I said. "And anyhow you can't enlist today. It's Sunday." Tom would be a soldier. He could get killed.

"I'll be old enough in fourteen months."

"That gives you time to play Joseph," I said dryly.

"All right," he said. "I'll be your dumb Joseph. But don't blame me if I forget my lines."

"Your line. You only have one!"

"O.K. I can manage that. I'm going home the minute the wise men leave their gifts. I hope it doesn't end before I get there."

It took me a minute to realize he meant the war and not the play.

Suddenly, I didn't care about being Mary or whether my hair was long or short. It didn't matter that I could toss it back and let it fall over my cheek in a seductive way. We were in a war with guns and bombs. I walked to the auditorium in a daze and found everyone in the same state. How could I act in a play on the day I found out Tom had to go to war?

"The show must go on!" Sandra Lee said dramatically.

We began fifteen minutes late minus Leonard, who

was one of the wise men. Sandra Lee walked on the stage, all poise. "Lo!" she said, "and to her a child is born!" She wiggled her shoulders so that her wings flapped gracefully and caught the light. Then, she turned to me expectantly.

Leonard's job has also been to bring the statue of baby Jesus from Jesuit's chapel but, like Tom, Pearl Harbor had wiped his mind clean, and a frantic call from Sister Maurice had sent Aunt Toosie rummaging in Sandra Lee's closet and Uncle Henry rushing over with the best they could find. Sandra Lee pointed to me and I laid her Shirley Temple doll in the manger filled with Spanish moss.

Joseph took a step forward onto the end of my blue cape. "Behold the Child!" he said, through Uncle Ben's beard.

From one side of the stage, the shepherds filed in, mumbling to each other, "Let us go over to Bethlehem and see this thing that has happened."

The shepherds looked at Shirley Temple and threw back their arms in surprise. "Glory to God in the highest!" they cried.

This was the cue for Norma Jean and the rest of the Heavenly Choir. They stepped out from the other side of the stage. I could hardly believe it was Norma Jean and not an angel! It didn't matter that angels were supposed to have golden curls instead of black ones. It was the way she held herself—tall and sure—that made her just right for the part.

"Glory to God in the highest and peace to men of good will," she said, her clear perfectly pitched voice filling the old Christmas message with new meaning. You could literally see the audience sit up and take notice.

With just those few words Norma Jean transformed "The Star of Bethlehem" into a message that brought Christmas and Pearl Harbor together. The Heavenly Choir burst into, "Oh, come let us adore Him" which was only supposed to be the end of Act One, but the audience rose without being told and sang with them. Clear and sweet, Norma Jean's voice could be heard above the others, as though the song belonged to her.

When we finished the last words, we got the biggest applause ever, and even though the play wasn't supposed to be over, the audience went on cheering and crying and cheered some more until Sister Maurice mumbled, "Best to quit while we're ahead," and pulled the curtain shut for good. Of course, they were really cheering because of how they felt about Pearl Harbor and our country, but it was Norma Jean who'd put it all together.

Sister Maurice walked out in front of the curtain and said, "Parents and friends, I won't keep you. We thank you for coming, knowing each of you made a special sacrifice to be here on this historic day that has already changed our world. I only want to say, the message of Christmas means even more on this Sunday. Dear friends, while our country is at war, may the peace of Christmas be in your hearts!"

I saw Tom walk down the stage steps and push through the audience. I thought he was hurrying home until I saw Louis and Aunt Mabel standing in the back. Tom said something to them, and then looked around. He seemed to be looking for someone else, and when our eyes met he smiled his nice smile.

Watching him as he made his way toward me, I realized it would take a life time to learn how to paint that smile in a portrait, and it came as a great shock to me that I was a long way from becoming a real artist. But I was sure, absolutely positive, that it was what I wanted, and for the first time in my life, I was truly pleased just to be Addie.

"Amen!" shouted Aunt Eveline from a long distance. I listened for more and distinctly heard "Snip! Snap!" The Communion of Saints line had just been cut. Aunt Eveline was moving to a new Heavenly address without a view of Audubon Street.